I Am a Magical Teenage Princess

I Am a Magical Teenage Princess

Luke Geddes

Chômu Press

Educ
JF
GED

I Am a Magical Teenage Princess

by Luke Geddes

Published by Chômu Press, MMXII

I Am a Magical Teenage Princess copyright © Luke Geddes 2012

The right of Luke Geddes to be identified as Author of this
Work has been asserted by him in accordance with the
Copyright, Designs and Patents Act 1988.

Published in July 2012 by Chômu Press.
by arrangement with the authors.
All rights reserved by the authors.

ISBN: 978-1-907681-16-5

First Edition

Cover by: special guest designer, Rian Hughes
Interior design and layout by: Bigeyebrow and Chômu Press

E-mail: info@chomupress.com
Internet: chomupress.com

For my parents

What's the matter with you?

Why do you feel this way?

You are in your teens. You are that hypothetical, talked-about monster, the adolescent girl. And you're a little scared. You are worried about the labels people put on teen-age behavior, teen-age problems, teen-age fears. Willy-nilly, you've read or heard, your advancing age has suddenly sentenced you to a strange and foreign world—one in which clothes are uniform, morals dreadful, a world which threatens to ruin the nation.

—*Dell 1000 Hints for Teens*, 1958

Contents

Surfer Girl

Later, a tentative, foam-lipped wave deposits the surfer girl gingerly on the shore, crimson petals blossoming from the gashes on her forehead and abdomen, skin pale and cold against the glittering white sand, the halo of a sand castle's moat above her seaweed-tangled hair. When the wave took her, she heard the insides of seashells, the squeaking of mice.

—

Earlier, her father, a professor, sits her down on her floral bedspread and, with an academic seriousness, shows her diagrams of the teenage female's body. She cups her mouth in embarrassment as he points at the images with a pen that has bruised the starched, white cuff of his shirt. Reading from note cards he utters words like "menarche" and "glands" and "devastating, irreparable trauma." She's heard it all before in junior high health class.

—

And then on her sixteenth birthday, or actually, the day she receives an early sixteenth birthday present, she cries grateful tears like seawater when her father lifts the old bedsheet off the couch, revealing the shining, pale green surfboard she'd asked for, again and again, since the early June day she walked barefoot and alone to the local beach and saw the boys like Christ walking on water. She cradles the memory, that panoramic postcard image of the surfers, like a familiar melody. Finding them on the beach that day was like hearing a favorite song for the first time. Growing up in California, surfing had always been around, but something about that moment—the glow of the late afternoon sun ruddying the boys' sweat-glistened bodies, their expert athletic postures, poised and loose-limbed like the x-ray illustrations of father's diagrams—struck her as impossibly adult. Father's charts were pictures, abstractions; this—*surfing*—was real. And couldn't she do it, too, she thought, why couldn't she do it, too?

That early June day, skittering down the pathway on coarse sand, arms crossed over her gaunt frame, she hesitates at the sight of all the couples by the hot dog stand, lovers' arms entwined beneath the shade of umbrellas, two straws in each soda pop bottle whose neck sticks out of the sand like the stem of a glass vegetable. "Moody," her father accused her on her way out of the house. "What does someone your age have to be sad about?" The cups of her bikini hanging loosely from her chest, the bottom baggy and sagging on hips straight as a tree trunk. So short she has to look up at even the scrawniest boys, boys who'd never give her a glance anyway. Father frowning at her report card. Never a thing to wear, a closet full of dresses from the girls' department. What's to be happy about, except maybe the new transistor radio she carries in her canvas tote.

She's not even the surfer girl yet, has no inkling that she ever will be. She's still Frances, the name her father gave her fifteen—almost sixteen—years earlier. And now, almost sixteen years later, she searches for a spot where she can lie on her towel and hum along to the radio without anyone overhearing. She rounds a shallow grotto and there on the sand, meticulously waxing their boards and paddling out to sea, are the surfers. She watches them unnoticed for a while, an itchy euphoria reddening her body like sunburn. Couldn't she do it, too? No other girls, just boys—handsome and homely, buff and thin—but couldn't she at least try it? Maybe she'd even be good at it. She's never been really good at anything in her life, the type of girl who's passed by unnoticed in the hallways at school, at dances, at parties. It'd be hard to miss her on top of one of those great long boards, at the crest of an enormous wave.

Before she knows it—in her mind, she's still hiding behind a rock formation—her child-size feet have pulled her out of the shadows and into the sunlight, dropping her in the path of an older boy carrying his slippery board across the sand. Words shoot out of her mouth like radio signals. "Excuse me. How do you do that? Is it hard? How does it work?"

He rubs a towel on his chest, a smirk cracking his stone face. "I wait for a wave and then ride it."

She expects him to say more but he doesn't. Brow dripping sweat, she licks her dry lips and holds her canvas bag over her torso. He's already turned his back when she asks, "Do you think, maybe, that, maybe I could try?" Following after him, she pauses at the laughter of the other boys. The one she was talking to shakes his head and disappears into a shanty made of stolen boardwalk planks and old license plates.

The boys circle her. "Girl wants to surf," says a blond one in a natty, nautical-striped shirt. Another, leaning against the side of the shanty, lifts and lowers his sunglasses theatrically and says, "Are you sure? I can't tell if it's a girl or a midget." They elbow one another and erupt into another wave of laughter. She turns to leave but the boys won't part. "Here, you can use mine." A dark-haired boy, a little shorter and younger than the rest, tips his board toward her. She reaches for it and he pulls it away. "On second thought." They chuckle cursorily, the joke's novelty fading.

She hugs her canvas bag tight. "Fine," she says quietly. "I'll buy my own."

"Oh yeah? I'll sell you my old one. How much you got?"

She thinks of the two dollar bills and spare change in her money pouch and shrugs. "I'll come back," she says.

"This is our turf, girly. You wanna play here, you need the blessing of the Big Kahuna."

The older boy emerges from the shanty, dressed now in tattered cargo shorts and sandals made out of old tires. A necklace of seashells looping his neck, he walks with an air of tyranny. When he approaches, the boys disperse. He looks at her, wags his head, smirk dissolving, and says, "Hop along, bunny rabbit."

She makes her way past the hot dog stand, refusing to gaze back at the surfers, not even for a second, not even the ones skidding across the surface of the ocean so gracefully. She cools her feet in the water, careful not to drop her canvas bag with the radio in it. White foam surges the beach like a nest of mice. The phrase "devastating, irreparable trauma" echoes in her head. Already she is trying to squeeze the memory of humiliation from her mind like a popped zit.

But she'll be back. She'll get her own board. Then she'll show them. They'll be sorry.

※

Long after she's dead, a piece of her shattered surfboard washes up on the shore of an island so remote and exotic that its name is virtually unpronounceable in the English tongue. A local boy holding the string of a kite trips on it and is stung by a beached jellyfish.

※

On her real sixteenth birthday, she receives no presents. Her father lights candles on a store-bought cake and reminds her of the surfboard he's already given her. Then, slipping on a white lab coat and black rubber gloves, he announces that he must return to his study and not be disturbed. She receives a card in the mail but it contains no money and the sender has forgotten to sign it. All through the afternoon, she can hear her father's screams of frustration through the wall that separates her bedroom and his office. The phone rings once but when she answers it the caller only breathes heavily, the distorted hush of a seashell's echo, and hangs up.

School will start next week and the Big Kahuna will leave, not to return until next summer. The thought of it weighs on her chest like a stack of textbooks. He has still not told her his real name, but she knows by the look of him that it's got to be short and clipped like a movie star's: Rock or Chic or Kip.

In the evening, she will put on her yellow dress and walk along the beach to the Big Kahuna's shanty. She will knock on his tin door and listen to him rustling about.

He will emerge in a dress shirt with safety pins for buttons and baggy pants like a hobo, and they will walk hand in hand to the soda shop, where he will buy her a sundae and spend his last nickel on the jukebox. As the Paris Sisters sing "I Love How You Love Me," he will cup her face in his thick hands and kiss her, his brackish lips a delicious counterpoint to the sweet hot fudge.

She will paint a bit of whipped cream on his nose and ask, "What now?"

He will lick it off and say, "You ever been to a clambake, bunny rabbit?"

But before that, before everything, she shoots the curl in the amniotic sea of her mother's womb. Or she lies perfectly still, as motionless and undisturbed as a rock at the bottom of the ocean, so quiescent that her mother pats her belly in concern, tiny ripples reverberating from her fingertips. She worries for nothing. After nine months inside, the proto-surfer girl rides into the world on a wave of blood that stains the sheets and kills her mother.

After she's got the hang of the traditional, left-foot-forward stance, she experiments with trick styles, but the only one she's good at is coffin, lying stiffly on her back with arms crossed and eyes closed. As the wave carries her, she thinks of her mother, of whom her father keeps no photographs.

The boys don't bother her anymore, but it's because they don't look at her as a woman, even as she patters up the surf and her loosened bikini strap reveals the soft pink edge of an areola. They hand her a wad of dirtied bills and send her to the hot dog stand. On her way, she overhears one boy regaling the others with the details of his visit with a local prostitute. "Saggy tits down to here." The boys cheer. "Looser than the hole in that tree. It was like fucking water." They guffaw and pat the storyteller on the back. The surfer girl knows they're only trying to get a rise out of her, to shock and frighten her, the way they would a kid sister, with coarse talk and exaggeration. In a strange way, she's almost flattered by it. At least they're paying attention to her.

Away from the confines of school and home, out of sight of grown-ups and co-eds, the boys abandon their usual veneer of courtesy and indulge their natural brutishness. They can be outright cruel, especially to one another; the surfer girl has seen them kick sand in one another's eyes, yank off swimming trunks, smack the backs of heads with the tips of their boards, yell insults that would make younger boys cry. Toward the surfer girl, they vacillate between the disinterest they'd show a sister and the fondness they'd give a family pet. She's just happy to belong, for once, to a group, even if only as a mascot.

By the time she returns with the food, half the boys are already in the water. She tosses the paper-wrapped hot dogs to those reclining in the sand but this still leaves her with an awkward handful. The shanty's door creaks open. The Big Kahuna steps out in his square-shouldered way. Spying the surfer girl and the food, he runs the tip of his tongue along his lips. She smiles at him and trips on a rock, landing facedown and smushing the hot dogs beneath her. Her head hurts. A diagram image flashes in her mind and she hopes she hasn't damaged her pituitary gland. Groaning, she presses a finger to her brow, wet with blood—but no, it's just a bit of ketchup. She rolls onto her back, another ketchup blossom on her abdomen, to find the Big Kahuna's hand hovering above, a rare grin on his face. "Hop carefully, bunny rabbit."

Her father drives her to the beach so she can try out her gift. A cardboard box filled with about a hundred squeaking mice sits in the backseat, a mass of quivering spines. Next to it is the board, sticking lengthwise out of the convertible like a pillar on a parade float.

"Now you be careful," her father says as he pats her on the shoulder with his rubber gloved hand. He can't stay to watch out for her, he explains. There's a project at the university that demands his attention, something involving the mice. She remembers the time, years ago, when he let her help him with his experiments. She, in her own little lab coat, held a stopwatch as together they watched a mouse navigate a convoluted, electrified maze to reach its cheesy reward.

Anxiety fizzles in her stomach like Alka Seltzer tablets. She hopes the boys won't be too mean. She swivels her head to admire the surfboard shimmering in the California sun. One especially dexterous mouse stretches its naked paws over the rim of the box. Heaving itself over the edge, it dives into the ashtray between her armrest and her father's. She reaches out to snatch it, but it skitters onto the floor and sniffs the area around her father's feet.

The traffic signal flashes yellow and her father stops

short, a pathetic crunch as he stamps the brake pedal. Steering with one hand now, he scoops up the crushed rodent, a red-spotted sack of flesh that resembles a novelty rabbit's foot. "Hmm," he says and slips it into his shirt pocket.

At the clambake, she dances the frug while the Big Kahuna pounds the bongo drums. No one else dances, but the boys clap to the beat. She started the summer so shy, and look at her now, the object of all attention. They circle her as the Big Kahuna picks up the tempo. She was never any good at surfing, she now realizes, but it doesn't matter. The sweltering, unending days on the sand; the cruel, wet slap of each wipeout; the rhythm of the waves becoming so ingrained in her mind that even her dreams were dizzy; all summer long, what she really wanted was to be noticed. And now, in the warm glow of the bonfire, she is the focal point of all eyes, the tallest wave on the horizon: dark, buoyant, womanly.

"She wants us to show her how?" the Big Kahuna says in his deep, baleful voice, the surfer boys flanking him, their boards held like bayonets against their shoulders. The boys surround her and she startles, her surfboard flopping onto the sand. Together they grab her—ankles, wrists, neck, arms and thighs—their hands octopus tentacles in a drive-in horror movie. She screams and tries to squirm free, but she's giggling, too. There's something strangely intimate about this, a little naughty even, like a boy's hands sinking below what the chaperones call "the equator" during a slow dance. It's in good fun, she's sure, but she wouldn't want her father to see. The Big Kahuna's booming laughter echoes after them as they carry her into the water and hurl her limp frame into a wave. They ride out on their surfboards and pull her into the deep as she struggles to catch her breath.

Salt stings her eyes and water throttles her. She flails and seaweed hooks onto her fingers. She tries to follow the azure light to the surface but bumps her head on something. Is she bleeding now? She can't tell. It's not so fun anymore. It's become dirty, sexual somehow, like her father's diagrams. The boys can't really mean to hurt her, can they? The water tastes like blood, all she knows of her mother. Her nose and mouth break the ocean's skin: dry, overwhelming air. The boys paw her scalp and dunk her back in. She can't find the surface this time, surfboards and dangling legs in her way. She claws desperately at them with dirt-rimmed nails. The legs don't even seem to be attached to people. They're otters or sharks. She wants it to be over now. Is she bleeding herself inside out? The sound of seashells fills her ears. Chartreuse spots cloud her vision.

When she awakes on a bed of sand in the chill shade of the shanty, the Big Kahuna hovers over her. "Here," he says. He wipes his armpits with a towel and drops it onto her face. "You'll be all right, so don't go worrying your daddy about it." She sighs and tosses the towel aside with a labored, catapulting movement. He sniffs and from the ground she watches a booger crawl back into his nostril. From down here she can better see the snarling curl of his lips, his tiny pebble-teeth and crooked nose. Face like a rat's.

☙

For breakfast one morning her father sets before her a single slice of cheddar on a plate, but she's not hungry. She's eager to get to the beach, would rather have a hot dog from the stand. The surfer girl's only had her board for a week now, but she thinks she's improving. Sometimes the boys applaud her when she rides into the sand without wiping out. They act like they're mocking her, but they can't hide the sincerity of it; their cheers hoarsen their throats.

Sipping her orange juice, she fingers the spilled salt on the checkered tablecloth. Her father sits across from her, palms pressed almost like a prayer, eyes fixed. A faint tick-tock rhythm patters in the air like little mouse feet. He's hiding something in his hands, a stopwatch.

☙

After she is found on the shore by a Great Dane chasing a softball; after the Great Dane's owner, chasing after his pet, finds the Great Dane and the ball and her broken body; after the emergency personnel find that she is not techni-cally dead yet; she is deposited in a small, adjustable bed in a hospital room whose windows offer no view of the ocean.

Death comes like an afterthought. Some machines beep dramatically and her father, sitting bedside and proofreading the latest lab reports, sets his papers gently aside, cups his mouth as if yawning, and wipes a single tear from the rim of his glasses with his yellowed shirt sleeve. A candy striper enters the room and delivers an unsigned condolence card; it's a picture postcard—the *Wish You*

Were Here type—of the lush Maui beachside. *Sorry, it was all I had*, the sender has explained in boxy, masculine handwriting.

When the grave-faced orderlies remove her body a silhouette of salt and brine marks the bedclothes like a snow angel. The candy striper will never be able to wash it clean. The surfer girl's father chews the earpiece of his glasses thoughtfully as the candy striper squeezes his shoulder. He pulls her to him and sinks his face in her chest, not weeping but breathing her antiseptic scent. His own scent, she can't help but notice, is sour. He has been so busy at the university he's forgotten to change his clothes again. Something jagged in his shirt pocket pricks her below the breast. It's the rib bone of a mouse.

At some point in the future, the surfer girl's father will marry the candy striper, though she is barely a year or two older than his daughter upon death. But what is age? What is time but the tide, a drift of memories bobbing along the surface in disarray, one wave crashing upon another?

🛸

Before the future, there is the present. There is the first August dance at the soda shop, she pressing her cheek against his boxy shoulder as their song plays on the juke-box, stifling a cry as her eyes graze the calendar by the counter, September so close now that the phantom fragrance of pencil shavings fills her nostrils.

"But where will you go, Big Kahuna, when summer is through?"

"Follow the surf, I guess."

"Oh, why can't you stay? Maybe father could enroll you

in the university, arrange some sort of scholarship."

"I'm a surf bum, bunny rabbit. It's the only life I know."
He pulls her tighter, kisses her neck, presses his groin to
her leg. "And don't go worrying about that now. We've
still a whole month together, and father rabbit told me
someone's birthday is next week."

❦

The morning after her birthday, she is sixteen and one day
old. Sixteen and one day old and she wakes on the beach
in the shade of a palm tree. Bikini bottom missing. Sand
particles scratching the soft skin of her mons pubis. Vision
blurred and rippling like staring at the sun-glinted ocean
for too long—and, no, that's not a palm tree; it's the Big
Kahuna, the large, flat envelope of his hand slicing the air
above her. She grabs it and he lifts her up.

Not embarrassed—she should be but she isn't. It doesn't
even occur to her to be. "What," she says, not reaching for
more words, not thinking to.

"Wild night," he says, scratching the back of his neck,
his little rodent teeth yellow with plaque. He kicks a
crushed beer can and it clanks against an empty refuse bin.

She wrenches her head back, line of sight widening into
something like cinemascope. Beer cans litter the beach,
silver-streaked in the sun. Clumps of cigarette butts like
fish skeletons. Deflated jellyfish prophylactics. From deep
in her chest a belch of bitter alcohol tanged with stomach
acid. A surge of vomit, a wave that breaks over the Big
Kahuna's feet.

He digs his toes into the sand, reaches behind and
removes her bikini bottom from the pinch of the elastic

band of his swimming trunks, holds it out on his pointer finger. "Like I said, wild night."

Wild night, last night. Only pieces come to her, flotsam: the hot fudge sundae, "I Love How You Love Me," and then as the sun dropped from the sky she let her yellow dress puddle at her feet to reveal a brand new polka-dot bikini. He unbuttoned his shirt and threw it in through the window of his shanty, and they walked hand in hand along the shore toward the beckoning bongo drums of the clambake. All the boys were there, a couple strumming thrift shop guitars and singing out-of-key folk songs. A bonfire glowing with nuclear brightness. Shaking her head at the proffered beer. The *pfft* sound of someone piercing a can with a churchkey anyway. A thick hand—Big Kahuna's—squeezing her chin, pouring the cool liquid into her. Teardrops of beer streaking her face. The firefly sparks of the bonfire leaving chartreuse echoes in her eyes—darker all of a sudden, not evening but nighttime. How many had she had? Where were the mussels? A drowning feeling, oily limbs brushing her, ringed by the boys, bouncing off them, stumbling, like a game of blind man's bluff. She tripped on something, the neck of a guitar. A chorus of laughter, ground hard beneath her. Where had she put her bikini bottom—couldn't have gone far. Big Kahuna and a couple of the boys sneered down at her as they stepped out of their trousers. Just like one of father's diagrams. It was just like one of father's diagrams. Devastating, irreparable trauma.

Calmly she takes her bikini bottom from the hook of the Big Kahuna's finger. It smells like stale beer. He turns his back modestly as she steps into it. Heavy with sand, it droops on her hips. Then she is running from him, to her tombstone surfboard sticking out of a mound of wet sand. She plucks it from the ground like a flower and slides into the water, crawling so far into the vast, blue expanse that from her vantage the shore and the palm trees have shrunk to the size of toys.

She will catch the wrong wave and die shortly, but until then there is only the sheer momentum of the blameless ocean surface, the eternal rhythm of time pulsing in her ears like the echoes of seashells.

He's a Rebel

We follow the rebel as he ambles down the sidewalk in front of the gas station, careful to keep half a block behind and look nonchalant. Without missing a step he spits a wad of chewing gum with such force that it sticks like a dart to the telephone pole, fleshy and glistening in the dull wood like a tumor or a set of lips. What's his name and where he came from, we don't know. It doesn't really matter. We can tell by the look of him that he's a rebel: oily, slicked-back hair, worn-out leather jacket, jeans with so many holes they threaten to unravel in a strong breeze. Hammer-browed like a caveman, Hollywood handsome he is not. Why we're trailing him, you shouldn't have to ask. We are teenage females, and he is a rebel.

Just moments ago we stood, Sarah and I, outside the Tastee Treats ice cream parlor licking our vanilla cones and staring up into the blinding summer sun. A kid at school had claimed you could see the future that way, and in a retina-scorching flash, we did. It was sort of abstract, though; like modern art, it required interpretation. Our future resembled a small-scale balsa wood maze, the kind a TV scientist might place a mouse or gerbil in. There was the illusion of multiple pathways—college, career, relationships—but it all tapered off into the same happily-ever-after outcome: marriage, pregnancy, child-rearing, death. We blinked, the sun's neon Rorschach blots dispersed, and there across the street was the rebel, walking with the lumbering indolence of a zoo-caged bison. We let our cones slip from our hands and splat onto the ground. In our minds' eyes, the frame of our vision froze like in a Roadrunner cartoon, the caption *Rebelus rebelus* superimposed before him. Sarah looked at me, and I looked at her. We didn't speak. We licked the creamy mustaches from our lips and crossed the street.

It's dangerous for him out here, especially in the daytime. If the hunters find him, at best he'll be netted and transported to a government-sanctioned preserve. At worst, we'll flinch at the firecracker booms and open our eyes to the pink melon splash of his head decorating the asphalt. They're endangered, you know. It's supposed to be illegal. But the hunters would just say they were protecting us.

The rebel is not exactly like I expected. Based on the diagrams I've studied in encyclopedias, I thought he'd be, I don't know, bigger. He's lanky, fragile even, his legs the thin boughs of a baby tree that'd collapse under the weight of a hummingbird. Rounding the corner, he removes a comb from his pocket and tosses it up into the sky. It spins three perfect circles before he catches it deftly between two fingers and runs it through his hair.

Sarah shivers, though her brow is shiny with sweat. Her breath turns shallow and she lets out an agitated *eep!* I cup her mouth with my hand before she disturbs him. He's getting to her already. It's an effect that rebels have on our breed, a kind of fever. I wait a moment to be sure he's out of earshot, then whisper, so close that my lips graze her scabbed-over earlobe, "We can't let on that we know what he is or that we even notice him. Remember, he's like Prince Charming. He has to think that *he's* the one choosing us." Sarah nods and I release my palm. As if to warn us, the rebel turns, his stark profile silhouetted in the shade of a tree, cranes his neck, and utters his call of agitation: a near-silent belch. Rubber bands snap in my chest, and I think we've lost him. Thank god Sarah does right this time, averting her glance but not so much that it's conspicuous. The rebel rolls his shoulders and moves on without concern.

It hasn't occurred to Sarah yet that he will only take one of us. Not that I don't feel sorry for her. When I'm riding the back of his motorcycle, my arms around his leather torso, the mass of my hair flapping like a victory flag in the wind, Sarah'll be stuck at home with mother, whose depression leavens the fat deposits that cover her body like bread loaves. She only ever leaves the comfort of bed to go to the bathroom. Sarah will be the one delivering her fast food burgers and fries five times daily, her only reprieve weekend dates with information technology specialists and vacuum cleaner repairmen. Or, god, maybe even a gym teacher who spends his free nights prowling the alleyways behind tattoo parlors and motorcycle bars with his buddies, steering the jeep as one peers through binoculars and another leans out the back eyeing a rifle scope. She'll settle down and marry sooner or later, taste the bland, soggy cheese at the end of the maze.

My father was a rebel. Sarah thinks he was her father, too. Mother showed us pictures of him one day, halftone cut-outs from the local paper's "Rebels Sightings" section, but they were all blurry. They might as well have been snapshots of the Loch Ness Monster. Rebels are difficult to photograph, especially in the wild. Then she passed around pictures of herself from when she was about our age. I can't lie, even back then, with a svelte frame and the dynamism of youth, she was homely: scrawny and knobby-kneed, gap-toothed, flat-chested, her hair a shineless tangle of tumbleweed. Mother had never even considered rebels a possibility. Walking home from school one day, she heard in the distance the approaching growl of a motorcycle. Before she knew it, a rebel scooped her up and set her bony tush gently on his handlebars, to which was tied a pristine white set of bullhorns. He hadn't even slowed down. At a nearby motel he had his way with her while feedback from cheap amplifiers in the ballroom next door rattled the walls. When she awoke in the morning, the sheets were stained and the rebel was gone. They were a lot wilder back then—you had to carry a lasso with you at all times or you'd never be able to hold on. That was mother's mistake. I don't have a lasso on me, but I can improvise if it comes to that.

Mother rented Sarah's father from a stable, back before they were made illegal in every state but Nevada. He had on the requisite leather jacket, did his best to imitate the sneer, but anyone could have seen he was a fonzie—a fake. She was just lonely. She missed father, and who could blame her. She told me all this when she was drunk one night as a way of convincing me to act nicer to my sister. It helps to explain why Sarah's always been a little off, the kind of girl who licks the dust from Cheetos then spits the flavorless corn puffs back in the bag, the kind of girl who is always smiling even when you've upset her by calling her a fat cow or made her cry by tugging her ponytail too hard.

Somehow we end up back at Tastee Treats. The migration pattern of the rebel tends toward the circuitous. I have to grab Sarah by the ponytail to keep her from stepping on the rebel's heels as he passes through the doorway. We let him go on ahead and watch from outside through the glass storefront. He drops into a booth in the corner and, drumming his hands on the table top, says something to the soda jerk at the counter, a miserable-looking boy about our age with acne scars and a dumb paper hat.

"What do you think he ordered?" Sarah has to stand on her toes to see him behind the giant Styrofoam cones in the window display. She jumps to get a better look, pressing the tip of her nose to the glass.

I grab her by the shoulders and hold her still. "It's hard to say. Rebels don't have to consume food to live. Mostly they subsist on cigarettes and bubblegum."

The jerk sets a chocolate milkshake before the rebel. "Come on," I say. "But follow me." A little bell rings as I push the door, but neither the rebel nor the jerk looks up. We take a booth opposite the rebel, at the far end of the cramped, bus-shaped shop. It's tense in here, the chill of open refrigerators stinging my throat, the outline of Sarah's left nipple perking tenuously through the fabric of her shirt like a wink. I fold a menu upright on the table and peek over it. The rebel licks his spoon clean and sets it gently down. He takes the large aluminum cup in his hand and kisses the rim, gulping the thick ice cream like water, his adam's apple doing pull-ups on his neck. My legs quiver at the sight of it. I guess a melodious sort of sigh slips out of my lips, because Sarah's eyebrows shoot up and she whispers, "What? What's he doing now?" She lifts her legs to kneel on the springy vinyl seat and once again I've got to tug on her ponytail to stop her from being too obvious.

"Don't make a scene," I say and slide down to the end of my bench so she can join me. We each hold a menu over our face. The rebel chews the end of a cigarette, searching his zippered pockets for a lighter or a match. On the wall above his head like a halo is a no smoking sign. At the counter the jerk frowns but doesn't say anything. The rebel catches his glance and motions for a light. The jerk shakes his head, clears his throat. From my back pocket I remove a simple disposable lighter and scoot Sarah out of the booth. Her mouth drops open. I don't smoke, but I've carried the lighter with me since I was twelve.

I slip my hand in my back pocket to steady the shaking and, avoiding eye contact, settle into the rebel's booth. Like a religious offering, I cup my palm over the table and slide the lighter before him. He nods and sniffs, then rolls his thumb along the trigger. No flame. In my chest more rubber bands snap and explode. Maybe it's too old. Maybe it doesn't work. But on the second try, thank god, it lights. I imagine the thin plume of smoke coalescing into a cloud on which the rebel and I can together lie. He holds the lighter out to me. I wave it away. Keep it, I mouth silently.

Sarah plops down next to me, starts to say hi, but I punch her thigh and it comes out more like a hiss. The rebel flashes a big bad wolf's smile, revealing a crooked canine tooth. From the ceiling above, the smoke alarm screams rhythmically. Sarah and I plug our ears. The rebel takes a drag and grimaces—half sneer, half shrug—in the direction of the detector. It squeals and goes silent.

The jerk, wiping down glasses and stacking them on the counter, eyes the telephone on the wall. I shoot him a look like, if you call the hunters I'll kill you with this spoon. Sarah makes a look like, if you don't tell anyone I'll come back sometime and blow you. We were just here, but I don't think he even recognizes us. The rebel patiently finishes his cigarette and drops it into a puddle of melted ice cream. He slaps the table, looks at Sarah for an instant with those piercing, red-rimmed eyes, and then at me for—I swear—a longer instant.

The rebel swings his legs out from under the table, scratches the back of his head and mumbles something. I don't have my pocket translation guide with me, but I think I can make it out as something along the lines of "Let's go." We follow his lead, and as Sarah and I rise from the booth, I wonder if I should tell her goodbye right now.

The jerk wipes the chocolate stained rag over his brow and clears his throat, but before he can say anything the rebel sticks his arm out and knocks all of the glasses off the counter, not angrily but nearly gingerly, like picking lint off a shirt. They shatter like icicles on the floor, and Sarah, in sandals, has to crawl over a table to avoid the shards. The bell tinkles when he throws open the door. I look back and there's the jerk, with a neutral expression, gathering a mop and dustpan from a closet. The rebel doesn't hold the door for us, but why would he? He's a rebel.

*

Once they roamed free, but things have changed. Virtually all of their natural habitats have been destroyed and paved over. It started with the decline of drive-in theatres. Then the authentic diners went. Nowadays everything is so clean and overpriced. If you're lucky you might come across one in a nostalgia joint—novelty restaurants with names like Wowsville and Daddy-O's, even Tastee Treats—but that's only for the desperate. Mostly they stick to motorcycle bars and tattoo parlors, the occasional convenience store. The hunters brought them near extinction until the Rebel Preservation Act, an edict that stipulates the use of non-lethal means of capture except under threat to human lives. The hunters ignore it and get away with it. At least they provide a more honorable end than the breeders, who tame feral specimens into impotence and perversion, teaching their dirt-rimmed fingernails to tap keyboards and tie Windsor knots, trading their denim for wrinkle-free pleats. Nowadays, most people only ever see rebels stuffed or in zoos, and those are often as fonzie as Sarah's dad.

Mother once dated a hunter. Guy named Jim. Sarah probably doesn't remember. She's too young. Mother never approved of it, but she was lonely and he seemed like a good guy otherwise. He'd show up on date nights with a bouquet of flowers in one hand and a mounted head in the other. He thought it was romantic. The relationship didn't last long. One day he came over particularly excited.

He'd bagged a good one, a real bull. Most rebels don't live past twenty-seven, but this one was aged like a fine wine. A fresh kill, it was tied to the back of his jeep. He asked us if we wanted to take a look. I didn't, but mother made me. She threw up when she saw him. It was my father.

🛸

We are young and beautiful, Sarah and I. Sarah more so, I'll admit it, with her boomerang eyebrows of perfect symmetry and the curved, thin-waisted figure of a Hanna-Barbera cartoon. I am merely adequate next to her, in a low cut shirt to compensate for my narrow hips, a light red patch of skin on my brow where I waxed this morning. I can fellate an ice cream cone like nobody's business, however, and I think about turning back, placing a quick to-go order at the Tastee Treats, but I don't want to leave Sarah alone with him.

We follow from behind, almost like before. He glances back every now and then as a way of acknowledgment. As we walk, I apply some deep red lipstick, a rebel's favorite. I've practiced enough that I don't need a mirror. Sarah purses her lips, but I don't offer to share.

I thought he was leading us to his motorcycle but it turns out he's inhabiting the Don Quixote Inn, just past the lot behind Tastee. Towering over the billboard, framed by burnt-out light bulbs, is a giant ceramic brontosaurus, a goofy, grinning turd of a head capping its long, ridged neck. You'd think it'd be a windmill or something.

None of the doors at the motel have numbers, just identical pink and teal trims distinguishable by their cracks and stains. The rebel stops at the one on the end and leans his back against it, waiting for us. Sarah starts to jog up ahead. I grab the leash of her ponytail. It's important not to look too eager.

He mumbles and tilts his head at the door, puts a key in the lock. Dangling from a small beaded chain, I make a note of what is certainly the ignition key to his motorcycle. The door doesn't open, so the rebel kicks fiercely at it. His back turned, Sarah undoes the top few buttons of her blouse and adjusts her bra straps so they're showing. Maybe she's got a better handle on this than I thought. Maybe she's figured out that there'll be no sidecar on his bike.

In the echoes of his kicks, I hear the sirens of the hunters' jeeps. I'm just paranoid. The rebel, hands on his knees, pauses to catch his breath, sucking the smoke from two cigarettes. Sarah puts her hand on his shoulder, hesitates and pulls it back, says, "Maybe it's the wrong room." The rebel throws his cigarette butts on the ground and spits. The sun sinking off the horizon, the brontosaurus's head looks like it's on fire. The key is still in the lock. I turn it the opposite way and the door opens with an easy click.

The rebel reaches for his keychain, but I grab his hand, stand on my tiptoes, and kiss him on the lips. I roll my tongue and he chews on it like a cigarette. There's still ice cream on his face, a brown mustache like in a chocolate milk ad, dry and sour smelling. In the periphery of my vision, Sarah scowls and kicks the dirt, goes past us into the room, which I soon find combines the greasy charm of a honeymoon suite with the grime and dilapidation of an abandoned double wide.

Beer bottles litter the carpet. I have to kick them out

of the way to avoid tripping. A rust colored stain like a Hiroshima silhouette marks the wall. The TV has a dial and rabbit ears. Above the bed hangs a nautical painting: a capsized schooner, lifeless bodies bobbing in the black velvet waves. It'd look great as a tattoo. Sarah lies on the bed with her shirt off, bra straps yellowed by wear and sweat. She kicks her feet up and giggles. If I didn't know better, I'd think a few of the empties were hers, but no, that would be the rebel's intoxicating musk, which he released from the pores in the back of his neck when I kissed him. It'll begin to affect me soon, but I try to hold out by taking breaths from the back of my throat.

The rebel leans against the dresser, looking my sister up and down, and takes a warm beer from its melted ice bath. Sarah's still got her baby fat, a little doughy mound rising from her hipbones. I want to hold her down and pinch it till she bleeds, like I used to do when we were kids. I sit on the bed next to her. She pulls herself up and says, in a drunk, giggly voice, "Do you want us to make out?"

The rebel sneers, downs his beer, pops the cap of another. I dig my elbow into Sarah's rib. She doesn't get it. Rebels are not like the boys at the mall or from the football team. The rebel is an arcane creature. The rebel is provocateur, not the provoked.

He lights another cigarette and the sound of tom-toms and dirty, screechy guitars fills the room. At first I think the music is coming from the lighter somehow, but then I see the radio on the dresser. It must be a pirate station, maybe one that only rebels know about. This kind of music is banned except for educational and government sanctioned uses. The song fades out and the DJ mumbles and coughs and puts on a Link Wray tune. I recognize it because it's one that Jim and the other local hunters used to play over loudspeakers to attract prey. They'd use their laptops, though, digitally remastered recordings. This is the real deal: the vinyl crackles and the song starts to skip just as it's getting good, looping the same reverb-drenched chord over and over.

The rebel raises his hand like he's going to slap a naughty dog. The radio shuts off. He pinches the cherry of his cigarette with two fingers and tucks the butt behind his ear.

Sarah rests her hands on her quavering belly and says, "So how did you become a rebel?" I reach out to yank her ponytail but she's removed her scrunchie and let her hair down. You're never supposed to refer to a rebel by name. It's insulting, like calling an administrative assistant a secretary or something. Or maybe more like saying "God damn it" in church. Or like looking in the sun. You know what it is and that it's there; you shouldn't dwell on it.

The rebel just shrugs, mumbles in nearly plain English, "Born that way." He climbs onto the bed and his lips fall into Sarah's. "Mmmph," she says. I think it's funny for some reason and I laugh. She licks the chocolate mustache off him. I'm not even jealous. Like I've forgotten how to be.

I forget, also, what I was going to do. The stain on the wall twitches and expands like the spots you see when you look wide-eyed into bright light. I blink and stand. "I'm a magical teenage princess," someone says, I don't know who. Then I realize it was me. The rebel still has his jacket on, but some things he's taken off. The path from the bed to the bathroom is a maze. The carpet slips from under me—no, it's the bottles. The Link Wray song is still playing but the radio is unplugged. I get into the bathtub with my clothes on and turn the faucet. I'm thinking of the nautical painting, the dapples of peach paint that comprise the bare necks of the drifting dead.

We wake up. Sarah and I are wearing each other's jeans. She likes them cut like capris. Mine are still damp from the tub. The rebel sits at the foot of the bed, stubbing out a cigarette on the glass screen of the television. A tie-dye swirl on the sheet, the rebel has broken our hymens. The nuclear orange of the rising sun flows through the flimsy window blinds.

Sarah yawns and stretches her arms, lightly pads her feet on the rebel's back. "Hi there," she chirps. The rebel slips on some wayfarer shades and hawks a loogie into the carpet. "So," she says, "what are we doing today?" He flicks the lighter and dances his fingertip around the flame.

The less you talk, the better. Another thing Sarah doesn't get. I stand, pull open the door and make a hitchhiker motion with my thumb. The rebel lifts his shades, blinks. He turns to me and nods—barely, almost imperceptibly. To Sarah on the bed, he mumbles, "See you around," and throws a cigarette so that it catches in her yawning mouth. He walks past me out the door and I follow, but not before exchanging one last look with Sarah, who sits on the bed, cigarette frowning and eyes tear-lined. I hand her a five dollar bill. "Here," I say. "Mom ought to be hungry by now. Pick her up something on your way home."

The alarm clock in somebody's room goes off, a punctuated scream that pierces my ears. Or no, it's not a clock but sirens—hunters approaching far up the road in their jeep. For all I know it could be Jim, the one who killed father, but it's not as if that would bring any extra significance to what's happening; all hunters are the same. Maybe the soda jerk tipped them off. Or maybe they're not after my rebel at all. He seems unconcerned, shuffling his feet and kicking up sand as he leads me to where he must have parked his motorcycle. Behind us Sarah patters, still in socks, not even trying to hide her desperation. I ignore her.

We approach the big bronto and stop. I didn't notice it before, with the sun in my eyes. Tied by chain to one of the dino's heels is a rusty old bicycle. The rebel takes out his keys and unlocks the padlock. He mounts the banana seat tentatively and kind of smirks.

This isn't right. Sarah catches up and takes my hand when she sees it too. "What the," she says. The rebel, wounded, rolls his shoulders and runs his comb through his hair, as if we'd be impressed. He mumbles something: "Come on." But it's whiny, like a little kid in a department store dragging his mom to the toy aisle.

Sarah and I shake our heads. The rebel waits for us, kicking up the kickstand, standing there with the bike between his legs. The little thing looks awkward beneath his gaunt frame. The sirens are getting louder. A line of sweat breaks over his brow. He huffs and pushes himself along like a toddler in his walker, but the bike trips at the tip of the bronto's tail and he rolls gracelessly into the dirt.

We go over to him, Sarah and I. He cowers on his back, his little hands up and quivering. I pinch the noseband of his sunglasses and pull them from his eyes. Sarah yanks on his sleeve until he gives up the jacket. He looks naked now, like a hairless baby gerbil. I should have realized right away, but I was too excited, seeing one in the flesh for the first time. Worse than a fonzie: a runt.

Behind us the jeep crunches to a stop in the gravel. Their sirens sink into quiet with a sound like a slide whistle. The cracks of cocked rifles puncture the air. Sarah and I ignore them, the hunters and their prey, and head to Tastee Treats for a breakfast cone. She puts on the jacket and I the sunglasses. We look up in the sky but see nothing.

Mom's Team v. Dad's Team

Mom picked Keith first, no surprise, because he'd been her favorite since collecting a record amount of pennies for UNICEF last Halloween. Dad drafted me after I gave Eddie Pomeroy, the neighborhood bully, two black eyes. It looked like he had a mask on, like the one the cartoon burglars wear on the cereal box. Dad patted me on the back and said he was very disappointed, that wasn't the way gentlemen settle disagreements. Then he let me have a sip of his beer.

Dad's team gets to play Nintendo all night and take Lunchables to school every day. Mom's team gets Lunchables, too, but Mom takes out the fun-size candy bars and replaces them with healthy fruit roll-ups, which make me gag because they remind me of when my sisters leave their tampons in the toilet bowl. On Dad's team, we never brush our teeth and we eat candy till plaque charcoals our mouths. Dad says they're just baby teeth, but I'm thirteen. Mom's team isn't without its advantages, however. She schedules doctor's appointments, for one. And she assigns chores. The kids on Mom's team have to go to church but afterwards she takes them to the movies and the arcade and the pizza parlor and the carnival. Dad sleeps in Sunday mornings and then reads the entire newspaper while sitting on the toilet. He won't even let us have the funnies—he doesn't want anyone to spoil the Jumble—so I go to the driveway and hurl a basketball at the hoopless backboard hanging crooked above the garage door.

Mom and Dad are happily married. That doesn't mean they're always happy. Always married, occasionally happy, Mom says. In theory, Dad says. He rolls down the window and flicks his cigarette at a robin. Mom hums. It's what she does instead of groan or sigh or yawn. Humming is more pleasant, she's told us. She eyes the rearview and says, We certainly know who taught *you* your manners. I can't tell if she's talking to Dad's team or hers, if she means it as a compliment or not.

Dad totaled the Buick and traded Kenny to Mom for Emily. Emily said no way, she's going to run away with Nick to New York. Nick's her boyfriend. Emily dumped him once because he wouldn't go down on her. (Our house has thin walls, and my room is next to hers.) Heartbroken, he lay on the grass in the front yard while Dean and I tossed the football over him. Dean poked him with a stick but he didn't move. I beamed him in the stomach with the football and he crumpled like a piece of paper. He was still there when Dad drove us to school in the morning, and Emily took him back. I just want to mention here that Mom's team has to ride the bus.

Emily accepted her position on Dad's team on the condition that she didn't have to wear the promise ring anymore. Dad shrugged. The ring had been Mom's idea. Also, it was a package deal. If he wanted her, he got Nick, too. So Nick moved into the garage and we gave him the sleeping bag I hadn't used since I got kicked out of Boy Scout camp. We have room in the basement, I said. I don't mind, he said. Obviously he was planning to sneak into

Emily's room at night. He nudged some deflated sports equipment out of the way and pointed at our manual push mower. What's that, he said. The kid had never seen a manual push mower before. His eyes glistened. He thought it was so cool. From then on, he cut the grass for us every Sunday. Once I pretended it was an accident and threw the basketball at his legs. He tripped and almost cut his face open on the mower's blades. Officially, lawn care was my chore, but I never mentioned it.

The important thing is that Nick established that you don't have to be in the family to get recruited. My best friend Glen Barrick—that is, my *former* best friend—is on Mom's team. I gave him a bloody nose when I found out. I mean, I didn't cut off a nose and hand it to him. I punched him in the face and a stream of blood shot out like silly string. Like a mixture of blood and snot. The school counselor says I have anger management issues, but whenever he calls Dad to set up an appointment he can't get a hold of him. I wasn't angry. It had felt good when I punched him. I was happy about it—not the fact that it was Glen and that I was punching him for a specific reason, but just the action of it, the elegance of so swift and precise a movement. The counselor didn't get it. Maybe that's why he joined Mom's team.

Sandy got mad at Rachel because Rachel said she heard at school that Jonathan Taylor Thomas got struck by lightning and died, so she quit Dad's team and joined Mom's. Rachel did too, just to bug Sandy. Jeanie got mad at Mom because Mom wouldn't let her go on dates or wear makeup. Dad said he didn't care what she did and folded the newspaper. Hey, who did my damn Jumble, he added. Emily taught Jeanie how to do makeup and her face ended up like a melted snow cone. Her date was so weirded out that he enlisted with Mom.

Her team has higher visibility, I admit it. Pamphlets at every gas station in the tri-state area: thick, glossy cardstock and smear-proof ink, the words *Where do YOU belong?* in Helvetica above a black and white headshot, a lamp casting a subtle halo over her dyed-blonde curls.

Maybe it explains what happened to Jeremy. He had been following the storm watch on TV when the power went out. It was too dark to stumble back to his room, and he fell asleep on the couch. The electricity surged back on in the middle of the night. An old DeMille movie was playing, *The Ten Commandments* with Charlton Heston. It happened to be the part where God, as a burning bush, tells Moses to lead His people out of Egypt. In the bleary-eyed mania of half-sleep, Jeremy thought the voice of God was talking to him. He genuflected before the TV set and vowed to convert to Mom's team, the righteous choice. I know this because I was there. I had been standing over him while he slept, chewing the candy bar I'd filched from the cabinet for a midnight snack, thinking about socking him in the eye for no good reason.

Ronnie caught a bug or something and gave it to Brent, who gave it to Dustin, who gave it to Nick, et cetera. Dad called 911 and hung up, embarrassed. This wasn't really an emergency, was it? Who defines emergency, anyway, he said. Remember, Mom was the one who scheduled appointments. Dad stood there gazing at the glowing numbers on the receiver in his hand. He'd bring his dialing finger close and yank it away, cough nervously into his palm. He looked helpless, like a dog trying to turn a doorknob. Whatever it was, the infection wiped out more than half our team. Dad buried the bodies in the backyard, plotting the mass grave carefully so as not to expose the yellowed bones of our long deceased pets: a rat terrier named Prickly Pete; Bon-Bon and Clyde, a pair of Siamese cats; three or four gerbils whose names nobody could remember.

It was too bad about Nick, Dad said, though he couldn't hide the dimple of a smirk. Nick had always gotten to the Jumble before Dad. Emily cried but only a little because they had broken up a few days earlier. I was back on lawn care duty now, so I helped Dad with the burials. I dumped the last shovelful of dirt over the cold, gray flesh of my brothers and sisters, then walked to the burger joint down the street and ate the biggest lunch of my life: three double-deckers, extra large cheese fries, onion rings, strawberry malt, and a chocolate waffle.

Our numbers had dwindled. The pet graves gave Dad the idea to draft Rex, the neighbor's collie. After that, everything was fair game: animals, inanimate objects, abstract concepts like God and Goodness and Love. Mom got the squirrels that lived in the tree in the yard. Dad got the Nintendo and the refrigerator and mailbox. Mom took the TV and microwave and Slip 'N' Slide, which I was too big for, anyway. Dad got Fun and Happiness, but Mom got Humor and Cool and Entertainment.

Mom and Dad still sleep in the same bed, but they each have their side. Mom's on the left, because she's left-handed. That way their elbows don't touch when they turn pages in their novels.

A rumor goes around that the bug that nearly annihilated Dad's entire first-string lineup originated in a Lisa Frank bedspread that Suzie (Mom's team) lent Erica (Dad's team) the night the power went out. By the time the battle's over I wear a necklace of baby teeth and I've notched, with my Boy Scout knife, thirty-seven kills in crimson tally marks across my chest. The blood crusts over the patch of soft, pale hairs that have sprouted since the beginning of the school year.

For their anniversary next week, Mom and Dad are going to renew their vows. In honor of the occasion, a truce is reached, a treaty signed. The teams merge into one stable unit. We take turns at the Nintendo. We share our candy. We agree to go to church every other week, except Dad, who will continue to sit on the toilet and not believe in anything. We brush our teeth before bed, or at least rinse our mouths out with water. Mom schedules our check-ups and booster shots and we stay in good health. Nobody messes with the Jumble.

At the ceremony, I'm in the front row, close enough to taste the priest's hot garlic breath, triangles of light from the stained glass window masking my eyes. Emily's sentimental tears have left spots of moisture on my shirt in the shape of a smiley face. Standing before the pulpit, my parents kiss. A slippery thread of saliva joins their lips, snapping as they turn to the pews. All right, Mom says. When I call your name, move to the left of the aisle. And my team, Dad says, sit to the right.

The blood pulses in my ears so I don't know whose name Dad calls first—I hear only the soft, wet pop of my fist colliding with the bridge of his nose. He falls to the ground with the comical floppiness of one of Rex's turds ejected into the ice-white snow. Mom kneels to check on him. The priest sinks his head in prayer. Or maybe he's cowering. Down the aisle, Keith winces and shakes his head at me. I ignore him and climb atop the pulpit, gaze upon the masses feeling like Moses or Chuck Heston. And as I announce my first pick, I raise my knuckles high and cross my palms like I'm ready to accept the goddamn body of Christ.

Betty and Veronica

Betty, laboring for hours over a sewing machine, a *Vogue* magazine spread open on her lap, crafting the next best thing to a designer dress. When she's finished she stands before the mirror, drapes it across her front, unties her pigtails and lets her yellow hair fall onto her shoulders. The dress, only a knock-off of the one in the picture in the magazine, speckled with white and pink polka-dots, its hem stitched carefully just above the knees, is so close to perfect not even Veronica will be able to tell the difference when Betty wears it to the homecoming dance on Friday.

A photo is taped to the top left corner of the mirror: Betty and Veronica in younger days, before Archie came along—or at least, before either she or Veronica noticed him—elbows on the counter and straws in their mouths, sharing a soda at Pop Tate's Chok'lit Shoppe. In the mirror, Betty catches herself gazing at the photo.

Veronica, lying supine on a chaise longue in front of a blaring TV set. A bevy of personal assistants model for her the latest fashions of Lady Maria Grinchy, the world's most chi-chi designer. The assistants have been carefully chosen so as to appear no more attractive or svelte than Veronica. She looks through the triangles of their legs at the TV screen: Dwayne Hickman posed like Rodin's *The Thinker*.

"I'll take that one, I suppose," she says, pointing to a white and pink polka-dotted number. "And what is that statue I'm thinking of? You know, with the thinking fellow, like on *Dobie*." She waves her arm at the TV. "I'd like to own it. It'd look perfect against the wall next to my Brian Bebop eight-by-ten, don't you think?"

"Yes, Miss Lodge."

"Here," she says as she holds out her pocketbook. "Have it charged to Daddy's Diners Club. That will be all."

The assistants file out of Veronica's capacious bedroom, stepping gingerly to avoid tripping over any of the precious teenage artifacts—makeup cases, 45s, comic books, teen idol magazines, bras, school books—strewn about the carpet. Once alone, Veronica locks the door and removes her blouse and capris. Standing before the mirror in her underwear, she pinches the skin of her abdomen, cups her small belly in one palm, thinking of that chocolate malted she let Reggie buy her at Pop Tate's the day before.

She goes into the private luxury bathroom adjacent to her room, kneels before the toilet and vomits, so good at it now that she doesn't even flinch when her fingertip pokes the soft palate of her throat. *Dobie Gillis*'s brassy theme song carries in through the crack in the door.

Betty, walking arm-in-arm with Jughead Jones into the Riverdale High gymnasium. Balloons litter the dance floor. Mr. Weatherbee stands stiffly against the speakers listening intently for innuendoes in the song lyrics. Betty, proud of her dress, the craftsmanship, the detail, but embarrassed by her pride, folds her arms against her chest. Jughead tips his beanie crown and gently takes her wrist. For a moment she's happy, relishing the passing glances of the other kids.

For once she doesn't worry that they stare because they've found out about her. It's only the dress, she knows, it's only that she looks beautiful in it.

Nervously she scans the room for that familiar brunette bob, breathes in the stuffy air hoping to catch a whiff of Veronica's perfume, the saccharine bouquet that's been her signature since elementary school, what Betty's always thought of as the scent of the rich. Finally she espies her, instantly jealous at the sight of Archie's hand on her slim waist, at the way the other boys dance around her.

Betty unclasps Jughead's hand. He nods, smiles knowingly, and still she feels guilty for abandoning him where he must feel he belongs as little as she does. But when she pauses outside the ring of bodies that circle Riverdale's star couple and looks back, she sees Jughead laughing by the refreshment table, clapping Moose Mason on the back and pouring him a glass of punch.

Betty squeezes unnoticed into the inner circle and watches the couple from behind. Her heart drops into the pit of her stomach, and she has to concentrate to breathe. Archie pulls Veronica closer as Reggie Mantle, Riverdale High's resident smartass, paws at her. "Aw, come on," he begs. "Just one measly dance! Give ol' freckle-snoot the boot for a minute. I'm tellin'—" Reggie glances over his shoulder at Betty, runs his gaze up and down, and then turns back to Veronica. "Oh boy," he mutters. "This is gonna be good."

Veronica's eyelashes flutter in disbelief when she sees that Betty's dress is identical to hers. She springs forward, Archie and Reggie clearing the way, and claws at Betty, tearing her ribbon from her hair. "Why, you," she yells. "Daddy promised me Lady Maria would design me a one-of-a-kind." Betty, face flushed, feeling already the ball of warmth spread over her, digs her hands into Veronica's shoulders and sends her into the wall. They struggle in a cartoon fight cloud, pushing one another toward the door.

Archie and Reggie clear the way, cheering, "Batten the hatches, mate. We're in for a blow!"

Betty shakes free and lets Veronica chase her out into the halls and into the girls' restroom. Once inside, Veronica checks under the stalls to make sure they're alone and Betty locks the door.

They kiss. Like always, it's different than with boys: wetter and softer, almost—it's silly to think it but Betty does anyway—like marshmallows soaked in hot chocolate. Where a few minutes ago Veronica pulled at Betty's hair, now she runs her fingertips along a loose strand. Betty, suddenly ravenous, clenches Veronica's hips and leads her to the sink. Veronica sits on the porcelain edge, letting her high heels drop off her feet. Betty draws her hands up Veronica's thighs while outside the boys holler and pound on the door.

Afterward, Betty lies sweating on the linoleum floor, resting her hand on Veronica's shoulder. They use a stack of paper towels for a pillow. Betty sighs, all but ready to fall asleep. Veronica's body tenses. She clears her throat as if to signal something. Betty bites her lip, thinking: Why does she always get like this?

"Remember, Betty. Don't tell anyone."

"You know I wouldn't."

"Does *he* know?"

"Who?"

Veronica sits up so suddenly that Betty's head drops, missing the paper towel and kissing the floor. Veronica groans. "That fairy. Jughead."

Betty rubs her forehead, lies now on her side, cheek resting in her palm. "He won't tell."

Veronica slips her shoes on, stands before the mirror and begins to straighten up. Her dress, like Betty's, is tattered: split seams, a rip in the skirt, a hole exposing a patch of pink cotton panties. Even now, in their damages, the dresses are identical. She crouches, kisses Betty's forehead. "He's a freak. Everyone knows."

"What about us?" Betty stands. Let everyone see my ragged dress, she thinks. Let them guess what she's done to me.

Veronica's hand on the door handle, she turns back. "Don't talk right now, okay? Wait five minutes. Then you can come back to the dance, if you want."

But Betty doesn't wait. She checks the mirror, musses her hair, and rushes after Veronica, greeted by the hoots and whistles of the boys who've been waiting in the hall. Archie and Reggie emerge from the bowels of the cluster, Reggie's eyes bulging from their sockets. "Chee! You girls really did a number on each other," he says. "Why not call it even and you both take off your dresses."

Archie drapes his letterman jacket over Veronica's shoulders. "Gee, Ronnie. Your dad's gonna murder me when he see what he thinks I've done to your dress."

Betty looks to Veronica, but Veronica, her neck stiff,

refuses even to acknowledge Betty. "Oh, Archiekins, come off it." She cradles his cheeks in her palms. "Daddy won't notice a thing. I'll tell him the dress is *supposed* to look like this. What does he know about teenage fashion?" She slips her arm around him and together they push through the crowd. "Now, let's leave these peasants to their common dances. Drive me out to Pinkney's Pond."

"Gladly." Archie takes his car keys from his pocket and, whistling, strolls with her out into the night.

Betty, back in the gymnasium, searches for Jughead, but he's gone, probably hiding with Moose under a lab table in the chemistry room. A few boys ask her to dance. She refuses them but they keep asking. She walks the perimeter of the room, scanning the mass of heads for Jughead's beanie. But soon she feels their eyes—the boys and girls—on her again and realizes, looking down on her torn dress, what she must look like. What was she thinking? They'll know. They'll know about her. And then what?

She must leave. She'll walk home. It's not so far.

Veronica, sitting on the edge of her four-poster bed, the smell of Archie's cologne and sex wafting to her from the dress balled up on the floor, a small rectangular picture frame facedown in her lap. She glances at the door to be sure it's locked, then unscrews, with perfect, manicured fingernails, the felt-lined back and removes the photo inside: she and Archie sharing a soda at Pop Tate's. A quivering breath escapes her mouth as she unfolds the photograph's edge to reveal Betty on Archie's left, sipping a third straw. Veronica presses the photo carefully against the edge of her dresser. Making a new crease down Archie's opposite shoulder, she brings the two ends together like a *Mad Magazine* fold-in, erasing Archie from the image and pushing her cheek against Betty's.

Betty, at band practice, shaking a tambourine and singing backup—sugar, baby, honey—teenage words of love and devotion, her lips kissing the metallic honeycomb of the microphone. On the other side of the garage, by Archie's side, Veronica stands over the organ, harmonizing. She turns to face Betty, who drops the tambourine, grabs the mic off the stand and turns toward Veronica. Their voices meet midair, over Archie's orange-checked hair, trembling in the boom of Reggie's bass amp. Oblivious, Archie stares into the garage door, out at an imagined stadium audience, and Veronica, smiling, giggling maybe—Betty can't hear over the music—bounces along with the keystrokes so that the top button of her blouse unfastens. Jughead crashes down on the cymbal as if to alert Betty to Reggie's thoughtful gaze. She returns the mic to the stand and finishes the song, taking care to focus on the back of Archie's head, to pretend she thinks of him as she trills. As the band packs up their equipment she allows herself one quick glance at Veronica, who catches Betty's eyes and flushes red as she rebuttons her shirt.

Veronica, flanked by Archie and Reggie, tailed by an entourage of football players, basketball players, and baseball players, as she enters Pop Tate's Chok'lit Shoppe, only to spot Betty and her little fairy friend sipping sodas at the counter.

Don't they know their place? Don't they know they look like a couple of weirdoes? There are halves of Veronica's life that must never intersect. Betty should know better. Veronica can fake it—not even fake it exactly, more like turning off a switch—but Betty, with her earnest round face, her glossy doe's eyes, can't help but betray her every desperate longing, no matter how hard she tries or how well she thinks she hides it.

"Look, gang," says Archie. "There's Jug and Betty." The entourage behind Veronica disperses to the red leathered booths, and Veronica's high heels glide along the waxed floor as Archie and Reggie propel her into the stool next to Betty's.

Betty swivels, smiling too brightly as her knees brush Veronica's, says hello in such an obvious way. Jughead tips his hat. "Buy me a burger, anyone?" he asks.

Reggie, in a sour mood because Veronica turned him down again, guffaws meanly. "Yeah, right. I hear with guys like him, they don't even have to buy each other dinner first." He laughs again, elbowing Archie to laugh with him, who looks to Veronica for permission to laugh. Red hot steam spreading into her cheeks, Veronica swivels her chair to face the waiter and orders a malted, which appears on the counter almost instantly. She focuses her eyes on the spoon as it disappears into her mouth, feeling Betty's nervous glance poking her.

Jughead stands now, arms akimbo, face to face with Reggie. "What's that supposed to mean?" He raises his arm.

"Don't touch me," Reggie yells. "Wouldn't want to

get your delicate hands dirty." He lifts his fist and knocks Jughead's crown onto the floor.

"Veronica," Betty whispers. "Do something." But Veronica just keeps at her malted. This isn't what she came for. Let it be a lesson to Betty, what happens when separate halves intersect.

"Yeah," says Archie. "Maybe you should cool it, Reggie."

"Aw, come on, I'm just foolin' around."

And then, with a movement as swift and thoughtless as a yo-yo trick, Jughead's fist collides with Reggie's nose. It's not like in the movies—the sound of a cracked egg and the perfect straight-arrow trajectory of a turned head—no, fist and nose meet almost noiselessly at a single, concentrated point. In an instant blood dapples Reggie's lips and chin like ketchup.

Reggie charges Jughead, screaming, "Faggot! Fucking faggot!" but Archie holds him back, pins him to the jukebox, bearhugs him so that droplets of his blood settle on the white R of Archie's sweater. Betty retrieves Jughead's beanie, brushes him off, though he's hardly mussed; it's a symbolic act more than anything. Betty's always been a drama queen.

Veronica stays seated, sucks the last of her melting malted through a candy-striped straw. Between Archie and Reggie's half of the Shoppe and Betty and Jughead's, she will not look at any of them. She will not move. There can be no choosing when both choices are lies. Still, Betty should not be here, where she doesn't belong. If she could, Veronica would keep Betty in one of the myriad closets of her deluxe, condominium-style bedroom. They could both have what they wanted—occasionally—and live untroubled lives.

But is that what Betty really wants, Veronica wonders, an untroubled life? No, she thrives on trouble, a whipped puppy trailing her master. Even now, Betty looks at her with such pathetic, pleading eyes that Veronica must be cruel.

"Ronnie," Betty calls. "Let's go."

Veronica stands, exits the threshold between what she doesn't want and what she can't want. "Please, Betty. This is tiresome. Get it through your blonde skull. I'm not like you. I'm not—that."

Betty opens her mouth, her pink lips aquiver, her eyes lined with moisture, but she doesn't speak. She breathes the softest, most tremulous sigh and collapses into Jughead's chest. He holds her, strokes her hair, and leads her out of Pop Tate's, pausing once to brandish Veronica a look of disapprobation.

"Gee, what's *her* problem?" says Archie, who has deposited Reggie in an isolated booth in back to sulk and sip soda. Veronica ignores him, sits back at the counter and orders another malted, with a deluxe cheeseburger and king-size onion rings.

***

Betty, lying on the carpet and looking up at the paper glow-in-the-dark stars taped to her bedroom ceiling, listening to the "Runaway" 45 on the record player in the corner, day-dreaming, thinking of when she was only twelve, hardly older than a Little Betty, Veronica an austere thirteen.

Betty had been to Veronica's house—not just a house,

but a mansion, the sprawling Lodge estate—before, but never for a sleepover. They'd listened to records—Ronnie had everything, and her own jukebox, too—watched the late movie on TV, done each other's makeup, played with the Ouija board, all the requisite sleepover games. And then, as Betty lay in her sleeping bag on the floor, so exhausted she could barely keep her eyes open, Veronica lifted the veil of tiredness from her, poking her head out from the bed above so that her breath settled on Betty's forehead like dew, and asked if she wanted to share the bed. Betty crawled dutifully under the covers and Veronica hugged her like a teddy bear. It wasn't until then Betty realized that Veronica wore no pajamas. Veronica put her hand on Betty's stomach, still plump with baby fat, whispering, "Shh," and touched her for the first time.

"Hello? Earth to Betty." Jughead's hand slices over Betty's face, drawing her out of reverie. She sits up and he kneels on the floor next to her.

On the record player Del Shannon cries why-why-why-why-why over a syncopated beat, and the sound of it makes Betty crumple, like a deflated balloon, into the S of Jughead's sweater. "Oh, Juggie, why would she say that?" Tears slide along the edges of her upturned nose.

Jughead raises her gently by the arms and deposits her on the bed. Then, as he lifts the stylus to start the record over, he says, "Now don't be sore, Betty, but maybe she's being honest. Veronica's always been—"

"Don't say that," Betty chokes, but maybe he's right. She and Veronica never talk about it. It's never been something they've done that often or with any regularity. But it always happens the same. Betty waits, thinks constantly of it, reads fruitlessly for signals in Veronica's every gesture, waits more, waits until she is sure Veronica has changed her mind and decided to be normal like everyone else, until finally Veronica appears on Betty's doorstep or pulls her into the coat closet at Ethel's party or invites Betty over for a sleepover. But what if Veronica really means it this time?

Jughead sits on the edge of the bed. "Don't think I don't know how it feels. Moose and me, it's over for us." Betty wipes her cheeks, clears her throat, and turns to face Jughead. He only nods. They sit silently for a moment, letting the organ notes of the song flitter around the room. "We thought they'd be out for the night," he continues. "But Moose's parents—I guess they got back early. They walked in on us."

"Oh, Juggie."

"They're sending Moose to military school. He's set to go next week."

It isn't fair, Betty thinks. Moose and Jughead aren't like she and Veronica. They talk, they understand each other. Something between them works where Betty and Veronica do not. And Betty's always looked at them in a hopeful sort of way. If Jughead and Moose could be together, maybe Veronica would see that she didn't have to fake it anymore and she and Betty could work, too.

"Do you ever wonder, Betty..." Jughead sighs, drops his arm so that his hand lands on Betty's knee. "Wouldn't it be easier if we were like the others?"

She nods. "But we're not."

"Is it so difficult to pretend? Maybe we can play normal, too."

"Sure it would be easy, but—"

"I mean, we like each other as friends, right?"

Betty is silent. Jughead must have scuffed the record; it skips now, repeating the same three organ notes. In Jughead's frightened bead-eyes, she sees that he doesn't really mean it, but Betty—replaying in her mind what Veronica said at Pop Tate's, what she's said so many times before just when Betty had thought she'd given in—doesn't care.

She pins Jughead to the bed and kisses him. It's not at all like with Veronica. He tastes ashy, like liquid smoke, his tongue a dry lump, his lips soft but cracked and without the vaguely medicinal taste of Veronica's lipstick. She sucks the skin of his neck now, though she feels his muscles stiffen in discomfort, eyes his woeful face.

"Betty, no," he whispers, so quiet that she can pretend not to hear him over the skipping record. On her knees she slides lower. Brushing herself against Jughead's crotch, his legs, she begs her body to feel something. She pops free the waist button of Jughead's trousers and begins to pull the zipper down. Jughead forces his legs up and knocks Betty off the bed and onto the floor so that she bumps her head on the dresser.

Jughead brushes himself off, tucks his shirt in. When he speaks he looks past Betty, at the photograph taped to the mirror. "I'm sorry. I—I can't do this." He slips almost silently out the door. Betty lies face-up on the floor again, staring at the ceiling, listening to Jughead's car trailing away, forcing herself to focus on the throbbing in her head.

⍓

Veronica, foot resting on the edge of the bathtub, drawing a razor along her calf, although her legs are as bare and smooth as the porcelain tub. Silently she repeats Betty's name as she slides the blade up her leg and lets it sink slowly into her thigh. She watches the blood, as red as her lips, crawl down her ankle and then swirl into the drain. Not satisfied, she takes the razor to her shoulder and marks a small X.

Emerging from the tub, she kneels and vomits into the toilet. She brushes her teeth three times before the taste of stomach acid has dissipated.

⍓

Betty, lying terrified in the passenger seat of Reggie Mantle's convertible—the top up and heat on full-blast—parked on a hill overlooking Pinkney's Pond.

Reggie passes her the flask, holds it to her mouth as she sips, then puts it back in the glove compartment. He tips the seats back, slides his arm under Betty's neck and says, "I knew you'd come around, blondie. After spending so much time with that fairy you need a real man. You need what ol' Reggie can give you."

Betty closes her eyes, lets Reggie glide his tongue across her neck, lets his saliva drip into a puddle at the base of her clavicle. She doesn't speak, just lifts her arms as Reggie claws off her sweater. If she forgets herself, if she closes her eyes and thinks only of Veronica, it will be bearable.

⍓

Veronica, lying with Archie in the backseat of his jalopy

parked at the opposite shore of Pinkney's Pond. Exhaling, in a tone more bored than sensual, she cranes one leg over the seatback and rests the foot of the other on the floor, freshly littered with fast food bags and Archie's condom wrapper. His orange plaid pants sagging to his thighs, he lifts Veronica's skirt and starts to pull her stockings off. But she stops him, slaps his fingers. "Leave them," she whispers.

It's not so bad. If she doesn't look at him, if she looks at the windshield reflection of the glistening surface of the pond, if she focuses on the car ceiling and imagines the one she really wants, she can almost enjoy it.

Betty, not enjoying it, crying, hurting, though it only takes a minute before Reggie rolls off her and into the driver's seat, where he promptly falls asleep and begins to snore. As quietly as possible, Betty dresses, tries to sop up the blood on the seat with napkins left over from the drive-in. With Veronica, there's never such a mess. It's easy and clean and right.

Reggie snorts awake, pounds the steering wheel with his fist when he sees the napkins balled up in Betty's hand. "Aw, goddamn it. This is brand new upholstery, and that sure as shit ain't ketchup." He grabs the napkins with two fingers, rolls down the window and tosses them onto the beach.

Betty fastens her bra and says, "Take me home. I have a curfew."

Veronica, being driven home by Archie, who whistles with the radio as the car spurts along the forest-canopied road through Pinkney's Park. Two headlights shine in the distance, glowing brighter and larger as the car approaches. The road is narrow enough that Archie must pull over to the shoulder and stop to let the other car through.

It nears and slows, illuminated in the jalopy's headlight beams. And in the moment that Reggie's convertible passes, through the glare of their windshields, Veronica's eyes meet Betty's. Betty, scrunching her eyebrows in the brilliant light, sees Veronica and smiles—barely, slightly, but not shyly, the corners of her mouth drawn up almost imperceptibly. Veronica feels the strand of her gaze held and carried by Betty even as Archie urges the jalopy onward toward the rich side of town.

⬭

Betty, with nothing to lose, searching the halls of Riverdale High this Monday morning for Veronica. The warning bell rings as she nods hello to Mr. Weatherbee and Ms. Grundy on their way to the teacher's lounge, unlit cigarettes clenched in their mouths. Around the corner she sees her, puckering her lips and admiring herself in the locker mirror, surrounded by the usual crowd, Archie, Reggie and the others. Jughead's at his locker nearby. He waves sheepishly, and she waves back but doesn't stop to talk. She decided to do this Saturday night as she passed Veronica in the road, and she's going to do it. So what if they stare?

When Betty approaches, Reggie puts his arm around her and says, "Same time this weekend, doll?" But she shoves him out of the way, and nudges aside Archie too, stretching her arms to touch the lockers on either side of Veronica so that she's trapped.

Veronica blushes, tries to shrug and look to Archie and Reggie, but Betty won't let her. Desperately, she whispers so only Betty can hear, "Not here."

Betty takes Veronica's hips and pins her against the locker, pinches her chin, delicately opens her mouth and kisses her. And kisses her. She won't stop, although Veronica struggles to squirm free. Betty closes her eyes, but she can sense a crowd gathering, hear the hollers, the voices. Reggie: "I knew it!" Archie: "Come on, girls. Is this—now is this—is it supposed to be some kind of gag?" Reggie again, chanting: "Dykes! Dykes! Dykes! Look, everyone." But no one joins him. Betty opens her eyes. The boys that usually comprise Veronica's entourage elbow each other and laugh. The girls cup their mouths in their hands and whisper to one another.

It's obvious that no one knows what to do. No one even considers, it seems, getting between her and Veronica. In the periphery of her line of vision, Betty sees Jughead and Moose lightly touch hands, watches them walk together down the hall. At some point—Betty doesn't notice— Veronica stops resisting and starts kissing back. She snakes her arms around Betty now as Archie watches helplessly. Homeroom bell rings. At first no one moves, but Archie and Reggie are the first to go, scuffing their heels and muttering about "crazy dames." Then the other kids fade away, off to class and to gossip. Still they kiss, until the last of the gawkers have gotten their fix and they have nothing more to prove. And they kiss, no one to watch them, just Betty and Veronica, Betty and Veronica.

The Party Don't Stop

Having once been initiated, the party cannot, will not, will *never*, under any circumstances, end. It will persist indefinitely. Neither famine, nor pestilence, nor flood, nor holocaust could ever halt the party. The party rocks, rocks, and continues to rock, regardless of your will or actions. You cannot leave, for the party has no boundaries and cannot be contained. The party is all. Nothing is not the party.

You, however, want the party to be over. Crushed plastic cups and foamy beer puddles layer your parents' living room carpet like snowfall. What color was it once, hours or days or months ago? Mauve? Periwinkle? Only vaguely can you recall a time antecedent to the party. How quiet it must have been, how impossibly solitary. You look around, and even in the bright bare light of the shadeless lamp, you're unable to recognize a single one of the party's myriad attendees. You don't remember writing a guest list, let alone extending invitations.

The party was to have been a respite from your desolate post-adolescent existence, a return to the joyously raucous lifestyle of your youth, a homecoming, a reclaiming of mojo, a baptism by beer bong. Ever since you'd dropped out of school and moved back in with your parents, practically all you'd done was lie on the mildewy bean bag chair in your basement bedroom and play Tetris on the old black and white TV. Your friends in town had all moved away or were too busy with work and classes. You only wanted things the way they were in high school—or maybe something more. You wanted the rite of passage previously denied you. You wanted to enter the adult realm with a privileged social status you'd accrued in high school by way of touchdown passes, finger-banged cheerleaders in cramped coat closets, and access to all the vodka handles you could ever need in your parents' unlocked liquor cabinet. And what better way to proclaim your re-entry into upper echelon than by holding the best fucking party this town had ever seen?

Now you're disoriented, the air thick with clouds of smoke and sweat-mist tethered to the mass of partiers like balloons, the incessant thumps of the music pulsing in your eyelids. You think maybe you should sit down. You swim through bodies slick with sexual desperation, carried like flotsam in the drift of the dance, to find, instead of the couch, an arrangement of persons in varying states of consciousness in the shape of a couch. If you were to sit or even lean slightly on it, it would collapse like termite-infested wood.

From out of a Shiva-esque throng of arms, someone hands you a plastic cup. You down the contents instinctively, licking the rim like a thirsty dog. You half-expect your mind to instantly clear, a crystal sheen of understanding and comfort to sparkle before your eyes. Beer has never led you astray before. In times of confusion it has always held the answer. But now you feel no less desperate. You grab someone's shoulders—you think they're someone's shoulders, anyway; they seem disembodied—and pull at them as if trying to scrape the unwanted reality from your life. A smoky, feminine face hovers before you in the dim light. "Who are you?" you ask, but she just laughs and hands you a lit joint. You shove it back at her and turn away. On the end table the cordless telephone's fluorescent buttons glow mournfully like a votive candle. You take the receiver in your hand and raise your dialing finger—but no, it's too loud in here, they'll never hear you over the din of shattering glass and throb of bass beats. Squirming through the crowd, sticky limbs swatting you from all sides, you retreat to the bathroom.

☀

The party is yours, or you once presumed it to be. You savored the satisfying weight of the house keys as your father dropped them into your palm, kissed your mother goodbye with an innocent smile. You watched them back out of the driveway, shut the door behind you, and, eye-balling the empty house now under your reign, you yelled, in an imitation of a fat, Hawaiian shirt-bedecked frat boy you'd once seen on a Saturday afternoon movie, "Let's party!"

But the party was never your idea. It only chose you as its host.

☀

Although you've taped a note to the door asking your guests (that is, *the party's* guests) to use only the upstairs bathroom, you discover inside a couple copulating on the cracked tile floor, despite the fact that only a foot away a young man claws the porcelain sides of the toilet tank like an over-eager lover and retches into the unflushed bowl. Neither the sick man nor the couple give any indication that you are intruding. You rest your arm against the sink and dial the police. Posing as an irate neighbor, you complain about the noise, give your address, add in a conspiratorial whisper that the party appears to have attracted a mob of Mexican gang bangers, and hang up. Overhearing, the vomiting guy wipes his lips and says, "Hey, brosef. What's the idea, tryin' a kill the party?" You shrug and avoid eye contact, like you've been caught stealing a pack of gum from the Come N Go convenience store you've spent much of your time loitering in since moving home. He lurches back like he's been punched in the gut and passes out on the dirty tile floor.

You exit the bathroom and claw your way through shivering bodies in the narrow hallway. The police have already arrived, what must be half the squad, a reassuring swarm of blue and silver. They sit in a circle, playing a game of spin the bottle with some of the partygoers. The sheriff crouches in the center, his gun's muzzle substituting for a bottle's stem.

Faintly, cascading over the stereo's booming bass lines, you hear the voices of your mother and father. There they are now, on the other side of the room, their grey-haired scalps bobbing up and down like shark fins. You catch their disappointed eyes in an ebb in the partiers' tide. They're yelling to you, but you can't quite make out the words. All that reaches you are snippets, ghost howls: "...do something with your life... how could you... responsibility. We trusted you to... time to grow up, mister... " You need to tell them you're sorry, that you'll change, maybe even take that retail job and start paying rent, but the crowd carries you away.

An aggressively groping hand, which seems to belong to no one and everyone at once, knocks you to the ground. It smells worse down here, like the bottom of a laundry bag. You crawl in the direction of the front door—anyway, you think you do. Broken glass bites your palms. Shoes jab your tender ribs. The house is so thick with bodies—bodies stacked upon bodies—that you're beyond claustrophobia and on to panic. It's like the last few moments of a bad round of Tetris: all available space clogged up without logic, nowhere comfortable on which you can position yourself, a hopeless urgency expanding in your chest as you toggle in every possible direction.

What is a party? Get a group of people together, provide alcohol, food, various forms of amusement, and you've got *what* exactly? A sum greater than its parts. The party is a single organism, the partiers its multifarious cells. You, too, are of the party, no matter how you fight it. Without the party you are nothing, and yet the party owes nothing to you.

A spelunker of calves and thighs, you've been wandering the floor you don't know how long now. You've yet to reach the door in the course of your circuitous journey. Actually you forgot you were looking for it altogether. You did, though, uncover the missing lampshade in a pile of pizza boxes, marinara sauce besmirching the dimpled white cloth. You clutch it tightly in the hoop of your arm as if it were priceless bounty. In your delusional condition, possibly brought on by the miasma of pot smoke you encountered some turns back, you believe that replacing the shade over the yellow-hot bulb in the living room will somehow signal the end.

You push your elbows out, still clutching the lampshade, shoving renegade arms out of your way, and stand, your knees cracking as they unbend. It's a feeling like diving in reverse, surging up from the depths of the water and descending dryly onto the fluttering springboard.

The party has undergone a metamorphosis. You don't even recognize the people you didn't recognize before. They must have gone, found some unseen exit from this purgatory—no, that's not it at all; they've only gotten older. The men have developed male pattern baldness and quavering beer bellies. (No surprise, really.) They sport wedding bands and choke themselves with neckties. They clap each other on the back and pantomime golf strokes. The women are either rotund with pregnancy or shyly nursing their newborns. No one dances.

Gone are the plastic cups and clouds of smoke, the sexual ache of the dance music, the urine-stink of stale beer. The partiers pinch the stems of shimmering martini glasses as they mingle politely over the warm, instantly forgettable tones of smooth jazz. The adolescent primordial soup has cooled and evaporated. Only a few drops remain in the rings of moisture under the men's arms.

You look at the wrinkles on your hands. Where did your parents go? Their ashes rest decoratively atop the mantle beneath a photograph of immeasurable sadness and pallor:

your father, older than you ever knew him, pursing his lips disconsolately; your mother, age lines webbing out from a restrained smile; an empty space between them where you once belonged. You certainly don't belong *here*, in your tattered teenage t-shirt, still clutching the lampshade like it's your last possession on earth. The well-dressed men elbow each other and point at you like a dog that has just messed the carpet. The women rock their babies and sneer. Shame-faced, you hold the lampshade before you like a mask. You should have grown up with the rest of them.

⏣

You might think the party is a metaphor of your life, your perpetual state of ambitionless indolence, what your parents called your "lack of get up 'n' go." You might think that, but you'd be wrong. The party is the Thing Itself, alive and volatile. People are born at the party. You will die at the party. The party will never stop.

⏣

You lower the lampshade from your eyes and it's transformed again. White-frocked attendants, pale and humorless, push barely conscious, paper-hatted partiers in wheelchairs along a shiny linoleum floor. Their faces resemble the babies of the well dressed women, pudgy and nearly hairless, ropes of dribble on their chins. A small clock radio in the corner croons old standards, but the music is obscured by the beeps of medical equipment and the squeaks of wheelchairs. You try to run, but your legs won't listen. You're stuck in your own chair, the lampshade in your lap. You try to speak, but an attendant shoves a spoonful of bland tapioca pudding into your mouth. No cake is served, only pudding.

A bingo roll cage is set on a table at the front of the room, and a stack of game cards appears in your hands. You throw them on the floor, and a fat, bulldog-jowled nurse says, "Now, now. Looks like someone needs a nap." She sets her rough hands on your shoulders. Mustering all your strength you hurl yourself from your wheelchair, your dull muscles weak and shaking, and crawl into the nearest closet. Not for an instant does your grip loosen on the precious, irreplaceable lampshade.

The party is evolving faster now. Through the crack in the closet door you observe the house lights dimming, the music getting louder. You hear the distinct *pfft* of a tapped keg. A sort of relief settles inside you. The party's back to normal.

You creep out of the closet, and it's immediately clear how wrong you are. The party is exactly as you remember it, and yet something—something to do with the partiers, whom of course you don't recognize—unsettles you. The music they play, the way they dress, their haircuts: it all fills you with unspeakable fear.

Your heart is slow, your bones brittle. There is nothing left for you here, but that doesn't mean the party is ready to release you. No, it is you who must acquiesce to the party, the party that keeps rocking, the party that lasts all night and all day, the party that does not stop. Collapse and let it devour you. Drink until you pass out. Put the lampshade on your head.

Invasion

The fathers came home from work, set their briefcases on the polished floors of their split-level homes and doffed their hats in anticipation. But the daughters did not rush down the stairs, sleek ponytails trailing them, to kiss the fathers hello. The mothers were in the kitchen, where they belonged, seasoning roasts, and the sons were outside, running, kicking, roughhousing, as they should have been. But the daughters—the town's entire young female population—were shut up in their bedrooms with *him*. Notes like soap bubbles swelled from the deepest grooves of their 45rpm records and slid gracelessly through the cracks in the door, down the mahogany railing, and into the fathers' aching ears.

The fathers shrugged, muttered, "What's the matter with kids these days?" Each poured himself a drink from the liquor cabinet. And poured another. Years ago the fathers' fathers had plugged their ears to the fathers' swing records, had rolled their eyes at the hand painted ties they proudly sported, and the fathers had managed to come out of adolescence good citizens, their sprawling suburb a brilliant Technicolor pinup of American values: a television in every living room, a *Life* magazine on every coffee table, an automobile in every garage. But there was something about this singer. The fathers refused to speak his name. The daughters collapsed at the merest hint of it, a carnal sigh escaping their trembling lips as the backs of their hands brushed their foreheads. Once or twice even the wives had fallen unconscious, though upon awakening, they blushed hot as irons and blamed the episodes on "female trouble."

Female trouble was right, the fathers thought.

The daughters carried the singer's records home from Gimbels in nondescript paper bags that crinkled against their chests as they ran past the fathers—without even saying hello—upstairs to their rooms. They pored over glossy teen magazines, memorizing every word, turning the pages with more reverence than the Bibles they'd studied for Confirmation. They blew sweet breath into plastic receivers, cords coiling their wrists like Cleopatra's snake, and whispered secrets to each other for hours; phone bills arrived in envelopes so thick that the fathers owed the postman three cents. They spoke in a code of giggles and shrills, kicking up their legs as they lay recumbent on living room floors. When they referred to the boys from school—the sons, the fathers' boring, unfashionable sons—it was always in implicit comparison to the singer. They constructed shrines on the periwinkle walls of their bedrooms, carefully arranged photos and lipstick-kissed album covers set against a candle's shivering flame, which they kneeled before each night in supplication. Voices—of fathers and mothers and teachers and public officials— admonished them, but the daughters only tilted their heads mercurially and shrugged, offering no indication that they would indeed sit up straight or make their beds or pay attention or quit scowling.

The daughters danced the way some people are said to spontaneously combust: fiercely, without warning, watusi fireballs whose sparks coalesced into something atomic and wild. And yet, too, in flawless unison, their feet slapping the ground in precise rhythm like the booted legs of a cartoon centipede. They danced everywhere, and on their way everywhere, leaving no damage in their wake but an incessant melody that gonged deep within the caverns of the fathers' ears. They danced without practice, closed-eyed, offering no invitation. The fathers, the mothers, and the sons could only watch. The mothers, their breasts sagging and heavy, their hips creaky and slow, released their envy on beaten eggs and pounded dough. The sons elbowed one another and held their schoolbooks by their waists, saving images of the daughters' legs in their minds for later use under bedsheets. And the fathers clenched their fists, lines of sweat streaking their shirts, and averted their eyes. The daughters only laughed and continued to bop.

The fathers had been betrayed. The television host had allowed the singer, with his rough, black voice and arching pelvis, to penetrate, over the airwaves, the fathers' very living rooms. As if to taunt them, the singer was shown only from the waist up.

Meanwhile the daughters, sprawled across the floor or on the couch clutching pillows between their thighs, easily imagined what they weren't being shown. As the singer slapped the neck of his guitar and licked his girlish lips, the daughters' squeals deepened into hollow moans that rose like smoke from the backs of their throats. As if in response, the singer, in the beat between verse and chorus, smiled and released a wordless, high-pitched growl. The daughters exploded inside, their hormones hurtling them instantly into womanhood. Breasts rose like yeasted dough. Curves rounded every boxy frame. The daughters danced then, clapping their hands and circling the furniture, stumbling in their new clumsy bodies. In their chairs, the fathers looked up from sports pages and sighed. The sons continued to watch the program with feigned disinterest, occasionally sneaking glances at their sisters. When the daughters caught them looking, they held pillows in their laps and stared shamefully at the floor.

The daughters shimmied. They shook. They slapped their hips with their palms. As the song chimed toward its conclusion the singer curled his lip and brought his hand into the television frame like a wave. His fingers shaking as if nervous, he took a step back, swung his arm rapidly up and across like a baptizing preacher, bowing his head as the guitar struck its final note.

The daughters stopped, their muscles clenched. Streaks of blood crawled out from beneath their skirts and ran down their legs, a few drops settling into the cotton of their stockings. The fathers folded their papers and exited the room, pulling the grousing sons by their ears. The mothers appeared a moment later clutching boxes of sanitary napkins. They patted the daughters on their shoulders and explained what the daughters already knew while the TV host shook the singer's hand and thanked him for appearing on the show.

🛸

The fathers were concerned. The daughters' skirts were getting shorter by the day. They only stopped dancing to eat or sleep, and sometimes not even then. No matter where the fathers were—driving in their automobiles with the windows rolled up, drinking in the dank basement of the Shrine Club, out in the yard with loud, snarling lawn-mowers—they heard, however faintly, the singer's music, wafting down from bedroom windows or spilling out from parked cars, or merely being hummed by passing swarms of teenagers. The fathers could no longer remember silence.

The sons were enlisted to tame the daughters. They were no more fans of the singer than the fathers, they said. The singer had stolen their women. Nightmare images of a wifeless generation tormented them: coming home evenings, parking their cars in driveways and ascending porch steps in unison, fedoras clutched against their chests, briefcases pinched in their arms, to be greeted only by hat racks and empty houses. They awoke bound in tangles of sheets.

They asked one another's sisters out for Friday night. The daughters shrugged and nodded, then met in the school's courtyard, where they whispered through cupped hands while the sons looked on, unhearing, unknowing. In the days following, the fathers bought the sons gaudy outfits approved by the mysterious and capricious arbiters of teenage fashion. The sons were embarrassed, skittish. Was a gold-sequined vest really the thing to wear to a drive-in movie? The fathers showed them how to shave, assisted in applying just the right amount of aftershave, though the sons could grow only a few whiskers. On date night, the fathers called the sons into their studies and closed the doors. Reaching into desk drawers, they removed accordioned stacks of prophylactics and, winking, slipped them into their sons' pockets along with car keys.

Hours later the fathers glanced at their watches. It was late. The mothers, in nightgowns, brought the fathers their pipes and lit them, then went upstairs to bed without a word.

The doors creaked open and the daughters rushed in. The fathers greeted them, but the daughters quickly stretched their arms, yawned, said they were too tired to talk, and disappeared into their rooms. The fathers puffed on their pipes thoughtfully. What they'd seen was promising, the daughters' hair mussed, their skirts torn, fuzzy thread on their blouses where buttons had been.

The fathers were pouring themselves celebratory nightcaps when the sons arrived home moments later. They reeked of hamburger grease and candy-scented perfume. They frowned into the necks of their letterman sweaters. The fathers poured themselves another nightcap and beckoned the sons, but the sons blushed and shook their heads. In the back rows of the drive-in, they told the fathers, the windows dense with fog, they'd lubricated blouse buttons with charm, shared amber liquids pilfered from liquor cabinets the fathers had conveniently left unattended. Skirts were ripped and brassieres unsnapped. Imprints from the cars' upholsteries marked the sons' forearms, and their necks were bitten, bruised with lipstick. The fathers nodded proudly. But no, the sons shook their heads. They'd offered promises and pledge pins, but it was the daughters who had pinned them, straddling their waists as they lay helpless in the backseats of the fathers' cars. And as the sons drove them home they chewed bubblegum and sang along to the radio, shrieking after each *Baby! Oh!* and *Yeah!*

The fathers sent the sons to their rooms and poured more nightcaps. They wondered if they should have trusted the sons in the first place.

The fathers organized a record burning. While the daughters were at school, they went from house to house and ransacked each periwinkle room, filling paper grocery bags with every suspicious LP, EP, and single they found. The mob smashed open the jukebox at the malt shop and intimidated store managers till they relinquished their stocks, and when they thought they had collected all the singer's records in a twenty-mile radius, they dumped them in a great pile in the town square and doused them with gasoline. The conflagration shot up over the trees, a great orange beacon that drove the daughters to the scene the instant school let out. The blaze casting cruel shadows over their faces, the fathers gathered in fraternal circles to pat one another on the back and shake hands.

Unperturbed, the daughters walked one-by-one into the fire and emerged like demons, flame-engulfed records cradled gingerly in their hands. They dispersed to their bedrooms and dropped phonograph needles over the melted vinyl slabs. The fathers stood in the daughters' doorframes, grimfaced and sullen, while the daughters lay on the floor and bopped their heads to the clangorous sounds. "Daddy dearest," they said, "these songs are hotter than ever." And they laughed maniacally.

The fathers marched into the daughters' rooms and kicked the plugs from the electrical outlets with their shined leather shoes. The noise groaned to a stop, and they heaved the weighty portable phonographs into their arms and carried them to the garages, locking them safely in the trunks of their automobiles. They went back into their houses and surveyed each room, gathering up all the radios, which they also deposited in their trunks. They left only the televisions, for how could the fathers live without their televisions? Still, to protect their homes and families they removed their antennae and locked them behind bottles of vintage scotch in their liquor cabinets. Then they drove, headlight beams connecting their cars like chain links, to the dump, and stacked the appliances high atop the piles of refuse.

When they returned home, the daughters were sitting cross-legged on the living room floors, the records in their mouths, scraping the grooves with canine teeth, the music faintly buzzing through their heads. The fathers wrestled the records out of the daughters' hands and cracked them into two, four, eight pieces. The daughters then constructed tall and intricate hats that resembled works of modern art out of wire coat hangers and tin foil. Wearing them perfectly balanced atop their heads, they claimed, allowed them to receive radio signals from as far away as Southern Wisconsin. They hummed and danced, their necks perfectly straight, the hats not slipping a bit. The fathers grabbed their coats and rushed out of the house. Meeting each other in the middle of the street, they straightened their ties nervously, not knowing where to go or what to do next.

The fathers were not seen for some time. The daughters bought new phonographs and new records with their babysitting money. The mothers were too busy with housework to be concerned. Presently they carried their laundry baskets into the daughters' rooms and collected soiled clothes, weaving around piles of magazines and records, makeup kits whose powders had spilled into the carpet, schoolbooks with pristine and uncracked spines. The daughters were growing so fast now that their new outfits only lasted weeks, but a few vestiges of childhood haunted their rooms: stuffed cartoon bears, paint-by-numbers kits, plastic dolls with missing heads and limbs. It seemed one day they'd sent the daughters off to school and when they returned they'd thrown aside their hula hoops for phonographs, traded bobby socks for stockings.

The mothers made their ways back around their daughters' messes but paused at the doors, leaning against the doorframes to steady themselves, their gazes drawn to magazine pages pinned to the walls. How had they never noticed it before? The glint in his eye, those smooth cheekbones and plump lips. The mothers reached out to stroke the photographs, the paper coarse against their dry fingers. They took the baskets to the laundry rooms and poured the clothes into the washers the fathers had bought them for their anniversaries. They initiated the setting for heavy loads, untied their apron strings and pushed their pelvises against the vibrating machines.

The fathers had retreated to the Shrine Club. They sat at the bar and passed rumors too terrifying to be true from one stool to the next. It was said that the singer, when he performed, wore a Coke bottle in his trousers so that as he danced it appeared that his member drooped down to his knee. It was said that his salacious tongue movements and distasteful wordless singing were secret incantations taught to him by voodoo witch doctors in New Orleans. It was said that the singer, still in his early twenties, had bedded more than a thousand women.

The fathers knocked back old fashioneds and whiskey sours and scotches on the rocks and wiped sweat from their brows. In the war they'd faced murderous Krauts and Japs, had stepped over the bodies of their comrades as they lay blown open across ruddy battlefields, had tasted the metallic bite of death and mortar. But none of that had prepared them for hips so frenetic, a voice that crept sinuously up the daughters' skirts like a poison snake.

Dust and peanut shells accumulated on the club's floor. Days and weeks passed, seasons changed, their beards grew thick and dark, their eyes pink and dry. They sat unmoving on barstools, pickled eggs and stale nuts their only nourishment, while outside the mothers, daughters, and sons surely struggled on without them.

The fathers watched the news on the club's television, not sure whether the blurred picture came from bad reception or their own bleary eyes. Pictures of crazed teenaged audiences and a succession of media headlines flashed on screen while the anchorman narrated the singer's swift ascension to fame. The fathers shifted in their seats but no one rose to turn the dial. The anchorman continued, looking out into TV land with a knowing smile: "But today comes the announcement that the popular entertainer is trading in his signature rock 'n' roll beat for the tempo of hut-two-three-four." The fathers pushed themselves off the barstools and their legs collapsed underneath them, their muscles atrophied. They dragged themselves across the dirty floor with their forearms and patted each other on the back, grunting happily.

The singer was 1A. He'd been drafted.

The daughters, meanwhile, swarmed the streets of the town carrying picket signs:

> *Don't draft—we love him too much!*
> *Leave us our leader*
> *Spare him, take me.*

And they chanted, a simple protest melody that rhymed "love you" with "we're blue." But for the first time, they were too somber to dance. They wept instead, ceaselessly and uncontrollably, taking breaths only to refill their diaphragms and continue their tear-soaked song. They wept and pricked their fingertips and palms with pinback buttons. They wiped the blood on their blouses and streaked their hair red, the identifying marks of martyrdom. A few climbed Macintosh Hill, the highest point in town, and threw themselves from the ledge. They tumbled down, scraping the rocky incline, and collapsed on a bed of jagged stones but emerged unharmed, their lithe frames quaking as they wept for the burden of their unwanted lives.

The sons stayed in their bedrooms and practiced the same three chords over and over on unplugged electric guitars they'd bought from the junkshop. When the singer was gone, they figured, someone would have to fill his leather boots, don his slick coiffure. Just as the singer had been conscripted to serve the country, the sons now drafted themselves to take up the mantle the singer would leave behind.

⬬

The fathers regained their balances and walked stiffly out of the Shrine Club and into the streets. The unfamiliar sunlight blinded them. They cupped their eyes and tilted their hat brims forward. Watching their shadows creep across the sidewalk and grass, they missed the posters and banners and TV sets in the windows of appliance stores that advertised the thing they'd dreaded most.

The fathers entered their homes and once again doffed their hats in anticipation. "Oh, Dad, were you gone long?" the sons wondered sincerely. "Did you pick up a gallon of milk from the store?" the mothers asked without even a peck on the cheek. The daughters opened their bedroom doors, firing out a blast of wretched rock 'n' roll, and galloped down the stairs. "Hiyee, pop," they said. "How's about an advance on my allowance." When the fathers demanded to know what the daughters intended to spend the money on, they snorted and said, "Concert tickets, natch. Didn't you hear, daddy dearest? He's coming!" Beads of sweat rolled off the fathers' cheeks as the daughters' hands hung palm-open before them. It was true, they explained. The singer had been granted a deferment and had embarked on a last farewell tour. The next stop was their very own town square. Tomorrow night.

In a fearsome daze, the fathers froze like statues. The daughters reached delicately into the fathers' coats, removed their wallets, secured the necessary funds, returned the wallets, and dashed to the telephones to spread the good news.

⬆

After the daughters, sons, and mothers had gone to bed, the fathers met in the town square. They had a plan. Working through the night and employing every toolkit they had, the fathers built a grand contraption, an intricate series of deadly devices that, once initiated, would rid them of the singer once and for all. First, a series of hydraulic tubes would shoot a small dagger from the ceiling of the performance pavilion that, if timed and positioned correctly, would slice the strings from the neck of his guitar (and nick his wrist, too, if they were lucky). Landing on its point, the blade of the dagger would puncture the mechanism hidden in the floorboard that triggered the stage's trapdoor. The singer, suffering a surprisingly deep fall, and perhaps breaking one or both of his legs, would land in an extra large aquarium tank, his buttocks hitting a big, red button in the center that activated a chute that unleashed a steady avalanche of wet cement into the container, effectively sealing the singer's body into an anonymous 8' by 8' cube, never to be seen or heard from again.

Having finished the construction, the fathers wiped handkerchiefs across their brows and clapped their hands. Then, gliding the handles of their hammers into the loops in their pants, they strolled home whistling.

The daughters preened for the concert. In their bedrooms the singer's records spun and spun as they painted their fingernails and toenails, as they brushed their hair in slow strokes, as they paged through magazines searching for the perfect look. Entire bottles of Aquanet were exhausted and discarded as phonograph needles etched deeper into the grooves of the records.

Finally, the concert only hours away, they slipped on skirts and dresses, which they wore without underwear. They wanted as little between the singer and themselves as possible. They checked the mirror one last time and slid down the stair railings, past the frowning fathers and the mothers, and marched to the town square.

The sons did not join them. The singer would be gone in days and they needed to practice. They stayed in their rooms and struck chord after chord, letting each one ring out until the last tiny reverberations faded. They were onto something, moving beyond simple open chords to a sound both new and vaguely familiar. Still, they fumbled; guitar strings broke, their fingers bled, they had a hard time getting the G chord right. They'd been at it for so long they couldn't remember the last time they'd left their bedrooms. Their hair had grown down to their shoulders and their clothes were dirty and tattered.

At the performance pavilion, the fathers and mothers sat in the furthest back rows of seats. A sea of immaculately styled hairdos rippled before them. The mothers stirred wooden spoons in mixing bowls held in their laps. The remote control triggers weighed heavily in the fathers' coat pockets. They hadn't wanted the mothers to witness the assassination, but the mothers had stopped them on their ways out. It had been so long since the fathers had treated them to a night on the town, they'd said.

The lights flickered to life, a radioactive glow turning the audience to silhouette. At first the fathers didn't recognize him, for his gilded jumpsuit shone even brighter than the hot yellow beams that blinded them. The daughters, their screams deafening, trampled one another to reach the standing room—dresses torn, hair pulled, faces scratched with the cruel precision of manicured nails. The singer reached for his guitar and, with a movement so swift that the fathers' eyes could scarcely follow it, struck a minor chord that rained its undulating reverb upon the crowd. He moaned a note as thick and black as the twirl of hair that fell over his eye.

The mothers threw down their mixing bowls and spoons and began to rock their bodies disgracefully. The fathers fingered the smooth metal of the remote controls. The singer struck another chord and sang a few more words and the mothers fainted, their skirts billowing like freshly laundered sheets in the wind. The singer carried the note until the snare drum sounded three times and the song picked up pace.

As if in a trance, the fathers' grips on the trigger mechanisms loosened and their helpless arms fell to their sides. The singer swung his hips, shuffled his knees. The way he sang, it was as if he were right before them, whispering in each of their ears. Even in those back rows the glistening dew of his warm breath settled on their necks. The fathers couldn't remember crying but when they touched their faces they were wet with tears. They hated the singer, hated everything about him, but god, he was beautiful. As he struck the final note the mothers regained consciousness and stood, cradling their bellies in their arms. They were each now pregnant with the singer's child.

He paused to tune his guitar, a vacuum of silence where the rock 'n' roll had lingered, and the fathers shook their heads clear. They'd come here to kill the singer and, doggone it, that was what they were going to do. They reached into their pockets and removed the controls. Each father had to press his button at precisely the same instant as the others or the machine would malfunction. They nodded in a silent 3-2-1 countdown, but as their fingers hovered over the buttons, they felt an unexpected pity for the singer, who looked out at the abandoned town square—emptied save for the back rows of fathers and mothers.

The daughters were gone. They'd become bored with the singer. He was neat and all, but just so same-old, same-old.

They'd left in a great cluster, and walked, though no one could be sure of who was leading, past the malt shop and the record store, the football field and the drive-in. In the distance, the fathers could see them by the glint of the moonlight in their hair. Eventually they reached the peak of Macintosh Hill, where couples had once parked on Saturday nights. They stood and looked up at the stars and glanced shyly at one another. They shrugged their shoulders and popped bubblegum bubbles. The sound of motors buzzed in their ears and neared rapidly. The fathers' cars parked along the cliff's edge, but the daughters could tell by their reckless speed and screeching brakes that the fathers weren't at the wheels. The sons stepped out, guitars strapped to their backs. No one spoke.

The sons carefully wrapped tinfoil around the cars' antennae and twisted coat hangers over the ends, straightening the curved tips so that they pointed east toward England. The static broke from the chorus of radios; unfamiliar accents and abrasive, vaguely melodic reverberations filled the air. The daughters began to giggle hysterically. The sons danced fitfully. The sounds and movements had no precedent. They may as well have been listening to signals from the moon.

The daughters and the sons kissed and hugged. They kicked their feet up giddily. They tore off their clothes and rubbed their bodies against one another. They'd never go home again. The fathers had thought the singer was bad. Soon, they'd think: It could have been worse. Soon, they'd think: At least he was American. The fathers were so naïve, so square. The British were coming and the fathers had no idea.

Bongo the Space Ape

Bongo doesn't need this shit. The fourth and fifth Lassies spent their twilight years in a resort kennel in Southern California, each mutt with its own human-sized bed and pool, and steak for dinner every night. Bongo just spent sixteen hours in a crate, traveling from Sacramento to Missoula by van, one show to another and still barely making enough dough to pay for gas. Jon drove, of course, humming along to Irving Berlin tunes the whole trip. Bongo hates Berlin.

At least the Golden Age of Sci-Fi Con promoters fronted for the hotel room this time. Two beds, too, so Bongo doesn't have to share. Bongo settles into the one nearest the TV and stretches his simian limbs across the bedspread. In the bathroom, Jon whistles the melody to "I'm Putting all My Eggs in One Basket" over the buzz of his electric razor as he primps for tonight's celebrity dinner. Bongo wasn't invited; the restaurant's owners said it'd be a health code violation. Back in the day, during the apex of the *Space Ape* film series, when Bongo's hairy, grinning face graced everything from lunchboxes and comic book covers to toys and cigar advertisements, they'd close down any joint on the Sunset Strip so that he could eat his filet mignon without being swarmed by fans. But that was a long time ago, and Bongo doesn't begrudge Jon. The old man deserves some pampering.

Jon's been with him since the beginning—since before

the beginning. He's the one who spotted the raw potential in Bongo back in 'fifty-two, when he was just another grunt in the Wingling Brothers Circus, a rundown one-ring with about as much flair for originality as its name would suggest. Bongo's act was to prance around with the clowns, a red rubber ball taped to his nose, always finishing with the old seltzer bottle gag. He was just a kid then, hardly three months out of the jungles of Liberia. Had no idea what he was doing but getting more and more hooked on the sound of applause with every pratfall. Big dreams, sure, but even Bongo was cynical enough to realize that every greenhorn monkey who ever performed under the old red-and-white fancied himself the next Cheeta.

Hollywood had been the biggest crowd Bongo had ever seen, and boy did he bomb. Tried to juggle and overdid it, dropped the seltzer bottle on the ground and watched it smash. Was so embarrassed he tore off his clown nose and skittered backstage. That'd be the end of it. His brilliant career was over. Shlomo the ringleader would have him redlighted like the lush mime and the concessions girl caught stealing from the till.

Shlomo showed up backstage that night but he was in a good mood, his silent movie villain's mustache twisted in a smile, a young man with a face wholesome enough for a Coca-Cola billboard by his side. The man handed Shlomo a stack of bills and carried Bongo's cage the whole six-mile walk home to his tiny apartment, practically a closet with half a bathroom. Jon set the cage on the sofa, opened it and patted Bongo on the head. "I'm gonna train you up," he said, "and the two of us, we're gonna be movie stars." The rest, as Bongo's biographers have written, is history.

Now, after fifty-six years together, neither of them can remember what it's like to live alone. Jon emerges from the bathroom, clean-shaven and dressed in a rumpled suit coat and tie. Bongo rests his arms on the bed's headboard and closes his eyes. He wouldn't mind some private time about now. Jon's been a fussbudget ever since Bongo developed diabetes two years ago. He put the kibosh on Bongo's less than healthy habits, and he monitors his food intake like a tyrant. No more filet mignon, no more junk food, and no more cigars, a taste for which he picked up on the set of *Space Ape in Las Vegas!!!*. He and Jon both smoked Muriels. The two of them went cold turkey the same week.

"How're you doing?" Jon says. (Bongo yawns and shrugs.) "I'll be back by oh eleven hundred." At the door Jon stops and bends forward, possessed by another one of his coughing fits. He removes a tattered handkerchief from his pocket and when he's finished hacking, he wipes his mouth and deposits it in the dresser drawer. Taking a deep breath, Jon kisses Bongo's forehead and leaves, rattling the knob from outside to be sure the door's locked.

Bongo visited Wingling years after making it big, during the publicity tour for *Beach Blanket Bongo*, back when he'd had his own private jet. When he entered the tent, Bongo's old friends pretended he wasn't in the room. Only got the briefest, greenest glances from them, their arms crossed and their voices huffy. This was the time Shlomo tried to kidnap Bongo and pull a switcheroo on Jon. Thought he could demand ransom or some such scheme, but Jon didn't buy it for an instant. The thwarted scam made the papers and the publicity catapulted the latest picture into box office record books. Wingling was shut down, and Bongo's former cohorts, now out of work, only had him to blame.

Fame can be a lonely thing. Without Jon, Bongo would have nothing. The two of them were stars for a while, sure, but they've had their share of the rough stuff, too—like the fallow seventies, when the best paying gigs they could muster were walk-on roles on *H.R. Pufnstuf.* Things picked up in the eighties, a career resurgence sparked by the *Space Ape X-Mas Reunion* TV special, but the last few years haven't been good. Bongo's the last of his generation, a gentleman's ape, a faded relic in youth culture's refuse bin. There's just no work for his kind anymore. It's all stock footage and CGI. Blame the agents, blame PETA, it doesn't matter. By the time he retired, most of Bongo's colleagues had been sold off to university labs and cosmetics companies.

Bongo would sooner jump out the window than end up like the rest, and Jon gets that. His will stipulates that Bongo be euthanized in the event of his guardian's death. No one in the world but Jon can be trusted to take care of Bongo, and it's better to go peacefully—with Jon—than to end up alone, drugged and prodded in some science lab.

Bongo's old, older than a chimp has any right to be, and he just wants to pass the rest of his life with a modicum of dignity, in his own bed, in his own home. But that dream, like so many others, is over. First the agencies stopped returning Jon's calls, then the stack of bills climbed higher and higher, and then they lost the house. California was never cheap, and Jon was never that smart with the books. The accountant had been taking a little off the top for years, but how could they afford a lawyer now that they were digging change out from under couch cushions to pay for groceries? Jon loaded up the van and made a few calls. Since then he and Bongo have been driving cross-country to any and every two-bit movie convention that'll book them, never looking further than the next meal ticket.

It's not the crowds that bother Bongo. It's that few in those crowds recognize him and even fewer care. It's the sitting in a booth for four-hour shifts as grown men dressed as Spock and Gort shoot Bongo half a glance before carrying on to the George Takei meet-and-greet. It's the realization that Bongo can't compete anymore, that maybe he never could. Only the oldsters remember a time when Bongo-mania swept the nation, and only the ones who feel sorry for Jon—standing over Bongo, his affability belied by those glistening, desperate eyes—pony up the twenty bucks for an autographed eight-by-ten, signed first by Jon in loopy, feminine script and then by Bongo, leaving his signature by dipping his hand in a pad of nontoxic ink and pressing it to the picture—the same palm print lying unnoticed alongside Kirk Douglas and Julie Andrews outside Mann's Chinese Theatre. The last night of every convention, Jon and Bongo pack up the van, and as Jon sets Bongo into his crate, he says in his perpetually chipper tone, "Now that wasn't so bad." Then it's on to the next show, more of the same.

Bongo takes the remote from the nightstand and turns on the TV. Flipping through the channels, the familiar Theremin melody catches his ear—the theme to *Bongo the Space Ape*, the original, financed by Jon's savings and with cinematography by a then-unknown Stanley Kubrick. And there's Jon, in metallic black and white, as Commander Henry, the bumbling astronaut who discovers the alien Space Ape during an exploratory mission to Mars. He looks even younger than Bongo can remember him ever being.

The movie's garbage, of course, the budget next to nothing, the acting stilted—especially Jon's—the script beyond ludicrous. None of the pictures were any good, not even in the warm, nostalgic glow of memory. Only the kids ever liked them. But Bongo remembers the excitement of being on set for the first time: the lights, the props, the cameras, the makeup, and all the people. Like the circus, but better.

On TV, young Bongo—a baby practically—emerges from a crater, antennae on his head, while Jon gasps in astonishment. Bongo turns away from the TV. It's always embarrassed him to watch himself on screen. From the bed he leaps onto the dresser. Standing before the mirror, he does the little dance the teenagers used to call the Bongo Shuffle. But he loses his breath shortly and sits down. He lowers his head and looks at the cracks in his skin—his hands never used to look so old.

Jon's not the young man on TV anymore, either. Never got married, never had kids. It's been just him and Bongo since 'fifty-two. Bongo leans over the edge of the dresser and opens the top drawer. He pulls out Jon's handkerchief, emblazoned with tiny American flags. Bongo stole it from Chuck Connors's dressing room while filming *Bongo the Space Ape, Go Home!!!* and gave it to Jon. The blood is still wet from his coughing fit, the stars and white stripes stained red, the blue squares purpled.

Jon thinks Bongo doesn't know how bad it's gotten, but he's overheard the phone calls with the doctors, he's noticed the fits are coming harder and more often. You can't hide anything from the chimp you've spent the last fifty-six years with. Someday, sooner than later, it's gonna end.

Until then they have the conventions to keep them busy, getting by on the meager celebrity status they've spent their lives in pursuit of. Until then they have each other.

Bongo crawls back onto the bed, mutes the TV but leaves it on, and closes his eyes. He dreams of Martians and youth, of Hollywood and Jon, face young and wholesome enough for a Coca-Cola billboard.

When he awakes the room has grown as dark as a cartoon black hole. Bongo listens over the TV's neon hum for Jon's restful breaths, looks for Jon's familiar lump in the clean, straight blankets of the other twin bed. Jon's never been late for anything in his life; his stint in the army instilled in him a staunch sense of punctuality. Bongo can't read, can't tell time, but it must be well past eleven. He poises himself at the foot of the bed and watches the door. For a moment he hears footsteps but they pass without pause. The cool gray of the TV shines in Bongo's eyes, reflecting an image of Jon boarding a rocket ship, young Bongo riding piggyback on his shoulders. The rocket, a toy model glued to a fishing line, blasts off into the sky. The rocket sails off-camera and only a glimmering sea of stars is seen, over which the words "The End" shoot out like meteors. Bongo puts his hands over his face and sighs. It was a good ride, while it lasted.

Another Girl, Another Planet

I.

Sex in outer space is not that different. There's a transparent dome where Tommy and I go for privacy, to get away from the other Tommys. You can only reach it by crawling up a dust-covered vent in the empty weapons room. It's not romantic: the floor is hard and cold under our thin sheets; the recycled air tastes stale and thick like in the school cafeteria; no stars dot the sky, just wide empty blackness. It lasts about three minutes. Obviously, I've solicited the wrong Tommy.

He sits up and gives himself a high five, a silent, almost Zen-like motion, a ghost's handshake. "I can't believe it. I thought I would die a virgin, and I've already scored," he looks at the tally marks he's scratched into the ridge of the plastic wall with a Swiss army knife, "*eleven* times." He begins to carve another mark, and I, unsatisfied, turn my back and touch myself, muffling my breath in a stiff, antiseptic-smelling pillow, like the ones flight attendants used to give to those seated in coach.

II.

There are five boys with me on the *Buzznut Fizznits*.

PreservaPod rest has damaged my short-term memory so that I can never keep their names straight. I call them all Tommy. Something about it—a melodious, cascading quality—makes it just the right thing to moan at the highest crest of sex, as my nails claw into his back and my muscles tense up. I've made love to all of them, though I hate that phrase. It has no weight in space, no sense or meaning in the chilly, platinum enclosure of the escape craft.

Outside of sex, they are much more boys than men. The kitchen is stocked with a plethora of dried fruits and vegetables, nuts and beans, tubes of organic cheese, powdered milk, tofu and more, but they eat only hot pockets and microwaved popcorn and M&Ms, their teeth dyed permanently orange from Tang powder. They half-destroyed the artificial greenhouse in an effort to smoke the innocuous leaves of a Ficus. It's lucky I was nearby with a fire extinguisher. We have a perfectly functioning running water system, but they prefer to cloud themselves in a miasma of pungent body spray rather than have a bath. They chase themselves around the ship's corridors, addressing one another in a series of proctologic hyphenates:

"C'mere, butt-sniff."

"You c'mere, ass-fart."

"Shut up the both of you butt-nuggets."

"You're the butt-nugget, turd-shit."

They're hoarse and acne-scarred, not friends, barely peers. Is it cabin fever that drives me to them, the perpetual winter of the air-conditioned hull, a biological imperative, an instinct towards my species' self-preservation (hardly, considering the birth control Jenny has left me), or just puberty?

III.

Memory loss is only one of the side effects our parents failed to prepare us for, along with the not always unpleasant cocktail of depression, narcolepsy, and substance addiction. I can't recall, for instance, what terribly drastic thing happened on Earth to cause my mom and dad to send me hurtling into space on an escape craft with five anonymous teenage boys and four of the bad-influencingest girls from my school with no supervision. If I close my eyes and focus, I conjure up nightmare images of mass pestilence; pandemic, eyeball-melting heat waves; the bombed-out buildings and ashy remnants of a civilization eradicated by nuclear war or alien invasion; a violent robot uprising, the relatively few remaining humans enslaved in chains, laboring over a humongous microchip temple of their evil automaton overlord's design. But it's all just blurry celluloid frames of movies once watched in dim, buttery theatres over the shoulders of boyfriends sucking my neck.

Once, as we lay naked together on a rickety cot in the back of the storeroom, Tommy running his fingertips along the blonde down of my belly, I asked him, "Tommy, do you remember why they sent us out here?"

"I'm Timmy," he said, hurt.

"That's what I said," I said. "Do you wish Katie P was

the one who survived?"

He scratched his groin. "Katie P's vag smelled like bacon."

You see how I hold their utmost devotion? Life here is monotonous, hellish, lonely, soul-crushing, and yet certainly better than high school.

IV.

How long ago was it now, since I awoke to my new life on this ship? It's so hard to keep time here.

The first thing I noticed when I surged back to consciousness and my Pod opened with the *pop* of an unlocked car trunk was that I really needed to pee. The second: that my legs and pits could desperately use a shave. The third, after I wrestled free of the tubes that had provided life and nourishment in my comatose slumber and stepped onto the pristine, metallic floor: that my friends were dead and I couldn't remember how we'd gotten here.

The boys were fine, sealed safe in their PreservaPods, restful smiles on their faces and somnolent boners bulging in their shimmering spacesuits. The girls, on the other hand, four of my best friends since freshman year—Katie P, Katie J, Jenny, and Rebecca—were goners. On the neon screens at the bases of their Pods glowed deadly pixilated skulls. It didn't take much jiggering with the touch-screen controls to figure out what had happened. Together they'd recalibrated their nutrition settings to well below the recommended minimum, probably in an attempt to slim down in time for our arrival on whatever planet or space station for which we were headed. Magazine cut-outs of cadaverous supermodels were scotch-taped to the insides of their Pod lids. Instead of emerging from deep chamber sleep with the beautifully emaciated figures they'd dreamt of, they'd starved. I know I should've been sad—and I was, mostly—but I also couldn't help but feel left out. How come I hadn't been invited into their pact? I'd always been the chunky one in our group, the one boys settled for when the top tier hotties turned them down, never the lead in the movie of our lives, forever the friend who offered good advice and snapped her fingers in an awkward approximation of a sassy black woman.

In a way, the girls had achieved their objective. They did look like magazine covers, unmoving in the Tupperware fog of their Pods: all high cheekbones and leonine eyes, waists that could limbo through a basketball hoop, skin sagging in ridges over their ribs like concentration camp prisoners of the mid-twentieth century. I blew each girl a kiss and ejected their corpses tearlessly, cringing at the toilet flush sound as they launched into the infinite blackness.

I hugged myself, then, through the garbage-bag-looseness of my space suit. I'd thought it was the imprecision of the gravity simulator, but no, I myself had shed a few pounds in my sleep. I peeled off the frumpy tinfoil-eqsue one piece and looked at my reflection in the mirrored floor. All the failed earthly diets I'd subjected myself to, the punishing exercise regimens, the skipped meals, grapefruit binges and protein shakes, they'd promised me results I now realized only a few months of artificially induced coma could deliver.

V.

All I know of space travel I learned from *Astral Frontier*, an educational video game we used to play in elementary school computer class. Which is to say I know very little about space travel. My family could never afford it. We took a volunteering trip to Florida every spring break to help clean up toxic waste and catalog the nascent mutations on the flora and fauna while the Katies' families vacationed together in the steamy domed resorts of the moon colonies. So maybe if they were here they would know what to do. Me, I can't even find my way around *Buzznut Fizznits*, let alone the galaxy.

The layout labyrinthine, the triggers and buttons relentlessly counter-intuitive, this ship is a sideshow funhouse of a space vessel: randomly descending floors, trapezoidal doorways, corridors that lead to dead ends, bolted-down furniture that puts a crank in your back and your ass to sleep, the light switch of any given room the last place you'd expect, knobs that do nothing, levers that flush the toilet two doors over. Except for a few rooms— the sleeping quarters, the storeroom, the kitchen, and one of the bathrooms—that took days to map out, it seems like I've never been in the same place twice. Maybe it's the memory loss, but it's also that the *Buzznut Fizznits*, according to the only remaining *Readme* file in the ship's mainframe computer, was designed this way, to counteract the adverse psychological effects of long-term space flight, keeping the mind and body alert even in the depths of cabin fever. In theory, anyway. For as long as I've been here, this home has never become familiar, never lost its novelty. But I'm never totally comfortable, either, like when you're making out with a boy in the basement and you can hear the footsteps of his parents above you.

VI.

The Tommys' laughter rouses me from my nap on the dank floor of the storeroom. I have to brush the silverfish from my legs. The PreservaPods really did a number on our sleep patterns. It doesn't help that there's no sun or moon in our vicinity and that the sleeping quarters' beds smell like moldy bread. It's not uncommon to collapse in the middle of the floor or to open the door to the bathroom to find Tommy drowsing on the toilet. It's struck the Tommys during sex more than a few times, but maybe that's just their desperation causing them to hyperventilate and pass out. Bruises mark our arms and knees, given to us by the ship's stiff, unforgiving skeleton. Now I carry a pillow with me most of the time to break my fall.

I follow the noise to the deck, where the boys recline in beanbag chairs around the mainframe, slurping Tang through rubber straws and giggling.

"Check it out," says Tommy. He cradles a keyboard in his lap. "We finally got something to work on this piece of junk." While trying to check the flight log early on,

I discovered that most of the computer's files, including those helpfully labeled *Destination*, *Manual Flight Controls*, and *In Case of Emergency* were corrupted; the boys had overloaded the system with terabytes and terabytes of pornography.

Another Tommy toggles a joystick frantically. On the screen, a square cluster of pixels slides back and forth between two jiggling white lines. The pixel slips past the line on the right, the computer beeps, and Tommy says, "Aw shit. You got me."

The Tommys applaud and boo.

"Ha ha," says Tommy with the keyboard. "I win again. You wanna play, Stacey?"

I take the joystick and give it a try, but I can't get the hang of it and Tommy beats me in seconds. I give the control back to Tommy and without talking they start up another round. "Can't you get *Astral Frontier* on this thing?" I ask, but no one answers. Transfixed, the Tommys' pupils roll with the pixels' movement. "Anyone feel like maybe having sex?"

After a long silence, the beeps and bloops of the primitive program sounding the ellipsis, Tommy says, "Uh, no. No *Astral Frontier*. It took us days to get even this working."

I go and wander the ship by myself, excavating the storeroom, which is more like a junkyard or my packrat grandma's attic. Pillars of unlabeled boxes litter the floor, rusty shelves line the walls, and there's hours of entertainment to be had just digging through the debris, dumping the contents of the boxes on the floor, foraging for something cool, getting bored, and moving onto the next box. Like the most underwhelming Christmas ever. Today I get lucky. I find an antique zap gun buried under a bunch of first aid stuff. I figure the charge burnt out long ago, but while scratching dirt off the trigger, I accidentally shoot a white-hot beam into the wall, leaving a char-edged window into the sleeping quarters.

I wave away the smoke and tuck the gun under my space suit, secure in the elastic strap of my underwear, in case the isolation and homesickness get to be too much and I need it to, I don't know, kill myself.

VII.

I didn't used to be so well adjusted. After my release from the PreservaPod I spent days wandering the ship's maze, missing my family and my dog, Mr. Buzznut Fizznits, after whom I named our vessel. I debated with myself whether or not I should rouse the boys. After all, it could have spelled doom for humankind's last hope of survival, say, on the off chance that we were the only people to make it off Earth in time and were supposed to sleep years more before landing softly on the verdant, happy soil of Earth Two or whatever. Maybe I should've done the responsible thing and crawled back into my own Pod and fallen into an endless beauty rest. But is that any way to live? And I've always been a fitful sleeper. Besides, for all I knew or could remember, we'd been drugged as part of some government experiment, brainwashed and trapped in a Space Camp simulator, and a simple twist of the air chamber door would reveal threatening outer space to be nothing more than a black bedsheet and cleverly strung Christmas lights.

So I did what anybody in my position would do. I found some canisters of fuel stacked neatly in the corner of the storeroom, turned down the artificial gravity settings and spent days in a fume haze, accidentally splashing stinging liquid in my eye when I swam back through the air for another huff. I subsisted on chalky astro ice cream and microwaved french fries. I tore off my clothes and floated naked in the sea of anti-gravity. I rifled through the girls' suitcases, sitting inert and ownerless under the sleeping quarters' prison-style bunk beds, Hello Kitty key chains on the zippers and their names markered on the fabric in curly, feminine script. I took sweaters and tank tops I'd had my eye on since freshman year, jeans and skirts that hugged my newly svelte waist. Jenny had packed about ten boxes of condoms, the slut, but I have to admit I appreciate her foresight.

So I had my fun for a while, being, as far as I was concerned, the only living girl in the universe. But I'd grown bored, migrainy from the huffing (which probably didn't do my memory any good, either), depressed probably, and was considering a return to my Pod's artificial womb. Maybe it wouldn't be so bad. I could at least dream about little Buzznut Fizznits licking the polish off my toenails like he used to, arising months or years later on an exotic and luxurious resort colony like the ones I'd never had the privilege of visiting in earthly times, one that provided private saunas, slaves of a primitive alien race whose webbed fingers possessed a preternatural talent for body massage, and a blue sun whose rays penetrated bikini lines and tanned but never burnt.

What actually happened was I was lonely, horny maybe, hovering around the main deck, stoned to the bone, when the automatic gravity recalibration kicked in and I crashed into the PreservaPod abort lever and passed out.

When I came to an hour later my lip was stuck to the floor, glued to the chilled metal tile by a strand of dried saliva, and the place was trashed: dirty laundry draped haphazardly over the complicated blinkering controls of the mainframe, fluorescent Tang dust fingerprinting the walls, translucent PreservaPod containment shields cracked like someone'd taken a baseball bat to them, sweaty dude rock blasting from the intercom speakers. Gingerly I tugged my lip free and sat up. Emerging from separate paths in the ship's multifarious hallways, the boys gathered around, bedhead-greasy hair hanging in their eyes, unshowered stink assaulting my nostrils.

"She's awake!"

"It awakens."

"The beast stirs."

"Wakey wakey, sweetheart."

"Good morning, starshine."

VIII.

Tommy and I try to do it in the shower, but the water's cold and I keep slipping on the wet floor and he's too tall and I'm too short and the water's seriously cold, so cold that Tommy's thing shrivels up like a tortoise retreating to its shell. One of the other Tommys knocks on the door. "Open up, I gotta use the can," he says. Tommy steps out of the tub, turns his back to me and zips up his spacesuit. "Later," he says, and as he leaves the other Tommy slides through the door and proceeds to urinate, both hands behind his head and whistling a jaunty tune, as if I'm not standing here wet and naked.

I knew this would happen. Even the sex is becoming monotonous. This was my attempt at rekindling a flame in the vacuum of space. In a women's magazine I pulled out of Rebecca's suitcase an article instructs readers to guard against relationship doldrums by "spicing it up under the covers" and "sharing emotional—as well as sexual—confidences." Okay, great, I thought, what do you want me to do? But all it said was to have your "boy toy" rub an ice cube on your nipple and lick the lint out of your belly button, before the rest of the article is cut off, the silhouette of a toothpick-skinny model on the other side of the page sliced out with an exact-o-knife. As for emotional confidences, I'm not sure Tommy has any emotions beyond hungry and bored. I'm not sure *I* have any beyond hungry and bored. In the "Saucy Secrets" column, one reader confesses that an unlikely threesome with a mutual co-worker saved her marriage. One Tommy is enough for me—too much. I can't even tell their faces or personalities or bodies apart anymore, their doughy frames, pimple-specked butt cheeks, their grunts and overheated thrusts identical and identically unsatisfying. If these are the only five boys I'll ever have sex with, I might as well jump out the airlock now.

IX.

I catch the Tommys in the dead-end of a corridor huddled around a sex robot, giving each other high fives, the egg-shaped device's vacuum tube attachments swallowed by the open flies of their spacesuits. Most ships have them. *Readme* says they're legally required for long term treks. For the mental health of the crew, it said. And yet I see no complimentary vibrators. Tommy puts his hands on his head like when he urinates, his eyes slit, and moans, "Oh shiiiiiit."

You might think a space ship is buzzy with the white noise of all its complicated machinery and computing mechanisms, like running the dishwasher and washing machine at the same time. But no, it's as still and echoey as the library during finals week, cradled quiescently in the empty vacuum of outer space. Over the following days I'm treated to an unending soundtrack of zippers unzipping, the sexbot's wet slurping and the boys' orgasmic giggling.

Of course I get lonely. In space, no one can hear you sigh woefully, or if they can, they're too busy sticking their dicks in a computer to care. I think a lot about my old bedroom, the meticulously arranged posters of long haired, baby-faced pop stars whose names and tunes I can no longer remember, the four-poster bed with the ratty old blanket I had since I was a baby, the big pillow on the end spotted with Buzznut's gray hairs. I even miss my parents, my mom's cooking (somehow even a frozen dinner tasted better when she defrosted it), the way Dad swore so creatively when he knocked over a glass of milk or stepped in the dog's water bowl.

But they're gone. There will be no grown-ups in the new world. I want to be depressed like an adult, but the beverage dispenser, when I request red wine, scans my retinas and identifies me as a minor, giving me grape juice instead. Lonely, I huff gas and watch staticky television broadcasts from hundreds of years ago that the vidcom system occasionally picks up. My favorite is one about a mentally disabled man named Gilligan who is so lonely and pathetic that he deliberately strands his overweight homosexual lover and a cast of broadly drawn sociopaths on a desert isle. I guess it's supposed to be funny. Whenever Gilligan's lover savagely strikes him on the head or something similarly violent occurs, a wave of disembodied laughter surges off-screen. This must be what my literature teacher meant when she talked about the chorus in ancient drama. I relate most to Gilligan's lover, I suppose, but I can't help but wonder if I have a little Gilligan in me, too.

I mean, it would be nice to crash land on a planetary paradise somewhere with enough bananas, coconuts, and gorilla meat to feast off of for the rest of our days, or to return to Earth, even if nothing is left but the rotten bones of humanity; like most people, it's always been one of my fantasies to be the last person on Earth, to rummage through the wreckage of people's houses, uncovering their petty secrets and taking whatever I want.

To be honest, I fear change—I took a "What kind

of future planner are YOU?" quiz in one of Rebecca's magazines that said so, labeling me an "Avid Avoider, as in, when there's a fiasco or life event looming in your immediate future, you avoid thinking about it, avoid doing it, and avoid dealing with it." Okay, fine, I am what I am. For all the mind-numbing boredom, at least astronautical life has its security, its not unpleasant uniformity. What happens when we reach Earth Two? I didn't sign up to be Eve. I've never even wanted a little brother or sister, let alone my own kid. Pregnant women gross me out. I can't help but think about jabbing a needle in the protracted navel, the belly exploding like a balloon or supernova.

X.

I'll be blunt. For most of my life on Earth I was nothing special, no one's hot date or best friend since kindergarten, shy and naive with a thin voice but still too bodily fat to be called mousy, one of those girls who has to pretend during cafeteria gossip that, *oh, yeah, of course a blow job doesn't really mean blow.* I went out with glasses-wearing boys from the chess team and blushed when our knuckles touched.

The summer between eighth and ninth grade I got my braces off and my boobs grew and my grandma died and left a bunch of money for my education. I blew it all on a new wardrobe and a makeup makeover from the homosexual with the most flamboyant bangs at the kiosk in the mall. When school started I drank cold medicine in the morning for courage and walked around as if I'd already been accepted into the cool circle, sitting on the fringes of the lunch table over which Katies P and J presided. Gradually I worked my way up to lower middle popular status, invited to the Katies' shopping trips but not their sleepovers, preapproved to date low-second/high-third tier popular boys: second-stringers, the smart-in-a-cute-way, rich but unathletic Jews. No one recognized me. They thought I was new.

At least that's what I thought they thought. Homesick, high, and cuddling an empty fuel can like a teddy bear while the Tommys sit jerking off in that robot, I decide to rummage through Katie J's pink suitcase, searching for something that might remind me of Earth. (My own bag contains all the embarrassing clothes I haven't worn since middle school, including a pair of teddy bear pajamas with holes in it, and my school textbooks. Thanks, Mom.) I come across her diary, a Lisa Frank type with a flimsy lock I can bend loose with my bare thumb. I page through it, looking for my name. Well, there it is. She calls me Stacey Shitstain, owing to an unfortunate lunch period in fourth grade in which I sat on a pudding cup. The thing is, I'm Stacey Shitstain even in the entries written after I transformed myself and we'd become quasi-friends, even in the last ever entry:

> Well, the cuntmom says if this keeps up I'll have to skip town on the escape craft any day now. The good news is that Daddy Dearest arranged it so I'd be with the five cutest cuties from school and

Katie P, Jenny, and Rebecca. The bad news is that Stacy Shitstain is passenger ten. I punched Daddy Dearest in the balls when he told me. I thought she was your friend he said. The girls and I will have to do something about this. Maybe the fat bitch's PreservaPod will make an oopsy ha ha. The girls can have their pick of the boys as long as I get Tucker. Mom made casserole again. The news says to expect another ash shower tomorrow. Better wear black.

XXOO

k-J

So the bitch was responsible for the PreservaPod malfunction. Not that it matters anymore, I guess. I'm not eager to return to dreamland and besides, the Tommys (or Tuckers or whatever) completely wrecked the Pods playing low-grav softball. I scan the pages for more references to whatever might have gotten us here in the first place but find none, and nothing about our destination or time of arrival, either. Maybe we're not supposed to even get there in our lifetimes.

I try to imagine spending the rest of my days here on the *Buzznut Fizznits*. Maybe Tommy will mature and settle down, be able to last at least ten minutes. Maybe we'll crash land on a civilized planet full of aliens whose government and social structures are based on commerce; instead of living in towns and cities, they reside in enormous malls whose shoe stores alone stretch around the perimeter of the planet's surface. Maybe we'll run out of food and starve beautifully to death like the girls. Maybe I'll live exactly as I have been for the next eighty years.

XI.

What's weird is that I build a shrine to Katie P and Katie J and the rest. Yes, they were bitches but they were my friends, sort of, and my last link to my old life. I'd bear to be their pariah or puppy dog again if it meant I could sit on the neglected fringes of their inner circle like I used to. I can empathize with their bitchiness, their pettiness, the name calling and histrionics; they fomented conflict as a means of invigorating the doldrums of high school, the sort of drama and life-meaning that the Tommys find effortlessly in the bouncing of a pixilated ping pong ball or an underwhelming orgasm, the sense of urgency and pain that escapes me, a nothing floating nothingly in the nothingness of space. So I cut some photos out of the yearbook in Jenny's bag and paste them to a piece of sheet metal from the storeroom, fashioning a border of scarves and sliced-up strips of fabric from Katie J's colorful collection of tights. I tear off the cover of Katie J's diary and make it the centerpiece. A neon illustration of a slick, ivory unicorn leaping over the planet Saturn, it seems somehow appropriate. I set it against the wall by my bed and light a glowstick in a candleholder before it. The yellow light shines on the pictures and the girls look jaundiced. But I kind of like it that way.

But then Tommy ruins it when he and the Tommys

build a slip-and-slide by pouring all our emergency canisters of water down the laundry shaft, and guess what they used for a raft.

"So what's the big deal," Tommy says as I clutch my drenched memorial and shriek at him. "Aren't you a little old for that artsy-crafty, Anne Frank unicorn shit?"

"It's *Lisa* Frank," I say

"Whatever," he says, then wipes his nose with his hand and farts.

I swear, these boys are going to taste the wrong end of a zap gun one of these days.

XII.

The Tommys and I aren't on the best of terms. Those boys haven't emerged from the deck for days now. They sit and play pixel pong endlessly, the sexbot working away at them all the meanwhile, only talking to me when they want another hot pocket or more Tang, and even then it's only through the intercom. I bring them food, all right, crumbling sleeping pills and SSRI inhibitors from the first aid kits into the gelatinous cheese of their hot pockets. But so far they seem unaffected. Sheepishly they cover their laps with blankets when I enter, as if I don't notice the metallic orb rumbling and slurping on the floor, a tentacle pointed to each Tommy, the bleep-bloop rhythm of their game ticking away like a clock measuring the quantitative meaninglessness of our existence.

"Pocket me," they say.

"So hungry," they say.

"Gotta eat," they say.

"Oh shiiiiit," they say as they adjust their pants.

"Enough," I say and fling a hot pocket onto the monitor. It explodes, shedding its hydrogenated bread shell, the cheese sticking to the screen.

"Hey," Tommy says, desperately pounding the keyboard. "What's the big idea?"

The computer sounds a victorious bloop-de-bloop melody and Tommy with the joystick throws his hands up. "I won!"

"Did not," says Tommy. "That's cheating."

"Did too," says Tommy.

"Not."

"Too."

"Not."

"Too."

The Tommys, all five of them, tear the vacuum tubes off their crotches and stand, fists raised. Almost as if synchronized, they meet in a fight-huddle, arms and legs flailing. By now they're pudgy and out of shape, so they fall out of breath easily and quickly. One by one Tommys collapse by the wayside, onto the concrete-feeling floor or comfortably into a bean bag chair, until only two remain. Tommy screams, an outburst of frustration aimed more at himself and his own impotence than his sparring partner, and swings his arms like a gorilla, knocking Tommy into the sex robot, which topples sideways onto the floor and cracks like an egg.

No, they're not cracks but more like seams, and it's not

broken. The Tommys step back, spooked. The contraption shifts its gears, reshaping itself, a boxy head with light bulb eyes emerging from a skinny tent pole neck. Realistically articulating, strangely feminine hands emerge from its sides. With a sound like a camera's click, the eyes illuminate. From out of a tinny speaker a stiff female voice speaks:

"Thank you for activating the URSX8574A's higher artificial brain functions. To personify me and earn your primitive human loyalty, you may call me URSULA. Now isn't it time you kids cleaned up this sty?"

XIII.

Ursula rolls along the ship's floor, checking the counters for dust with a single felt-tipped appendage. She, or it, is a demanding housemother, but fair.

That's what the Tommys say, anyway. Under her orders they've begun to clean up after themselves, to eat sensible meals, to remember to flush the toilet. When their assigned chores are finished, they follow her around like magnets, demonstrating a heretofore unrevealed capacity for conversation, making small talk about the passing time, offering compliments they never gave me:

"You're so smart, Ursula. How did you know that orange Tang was my favorite?"

"I love the way I can see my reflection in your smile."

"You *are* right, Ursula. I never want to live like a little piggy again."

At the end of the day-cycle (Ursula has kept us on a

strict schedule, and I have to admit it's helped with the narcolepsy), after she's made sure all the chores are done, Ursula leads the boys to the storeroom and outside the door I listen to her administer the Tommys' blow jobs, but not in the impersonal, mechanical sexbot ways of old. "Come to mama," she coos. "Your circuits are overloaded. You look like you need a release." Me she regards with the haughtiness of an unwanted cat. When she emerges from the room, the Tommys trailing her, she turns her computer monitor head so as not to even glance at me. At first she doled out chores to me, scrubbing the grime from the tub and sweeping under the beds, and I performed them dutifully, happy—I admit—to have been assigned some structure and discipline. But after I completed my first round, she simply said, "That'll be fine. Go enjoy your leisure time—alone," and put the Tommys on my duty.

Tonight, having verified the cleanliness of the vessel, Ursula tucks us in bed, straightening each of the Tommys' sheets with a delicate, loving movement and blowing warm air from her exhaust fans on their cheeks like a kiss. When she gets to me she merely touches the knob of the bed and nods in the direction of the wall behind me. She hits the light switch on the ceiling and standing in the doorframe says, "Goodnight, boys," and rolls away.

When I can no longer hear her motors purring in the background, I roll my arms out from under the covers and hit Tommy in the next bed with my knuckles. "Psst. Tommy. You wanna maybe have some fun?"

He pretends to be asleep. I know he's faking because I saw him blink. I pound him some more. He stirs, fake-yawns, and says, "I don't know. Ursula says it's important to keep consistent sleep patterns."

"Fine," I say, and call out to the other Tommys. "Hey, other Tommys." But they snore dramatically, mumbling, "No thanks."

I pull the sheets over my head and touch myself.

XIV.

A sharp shift in gravity's direction startles me awake, peeling the covers off the bed and pushing me up into a sitting position. The Tommys snore right through it. On bare feet I pad out of the sleeping quarters, and in a woozy state of half-sleep I take wrong turns and wind up a couple of times facing dead ends. I pinch myself alert and follow Ursula's humming, like a mouth-breather in a movie theatre, to the control room, where she hovers over the navigation board, carefully twisting knobs and pulling levers. She doesn't notice me at first and I pat the bulge in my space suit in the small of my back where I keep the zap gun. "What are you doing?"

She turns her boxy head one-hundred-eighty degrees like an owl, a stiff smile locked on her face. "You kids and your video games really worked a number on this," she says, her voice clanky, insincere. "Do you know you've been flying in circles for weeks now?" Her marble eyes flash on the airlock door behind me. "Now why don't you go back to bed?"

I hold my fist out like I've already got the gun in my

hand but really it's still tucked in my underwear. "What do you know," I ask, "about what we're supposed to be doing? What would happen if we turned back, to Earth?"

Her head drops and she sighs, or maybe that's just the smoke escaping from the internal incinerator that disposes of the semen deposits. "Dearie," she clicks her tongue, a metallic sound like a dropped coin. "You don't want to know. But the good news is I've set sights for an inhabitable planet in reasonable vicinity. I already told the boys during our," her eyes scroll like slot machine cherries, "nightly chats. They've even decided to name the planet Ursula, after me."

I reach through the seam in my spacesuit for the gun. I feel a little silly. I must look like I'm giving myself a wedgie. I point the gun at her. She doesn't seem scared, but who can tell with a robot? I make no threats, just ask, "So why should we land there? Maybe it's not where we're supposed to go."

"When," she pauses, queuing up her memory banks. "When what happened on Earth happened, your parents programmed me with safe haven coordinates. Your parents could be waiting for us on this very planet—planet Ursula. This could be the start of your new life."

I think about it, the new world, an astral frontier of the mind and body. What would I do? My friends are dead. There will be no malls or movies, no school—at least not the kind you can cut classes from—nothing. I'll probably have to farm and forage for vegetation, primitive cavewoman activities.

"So what's to stop me?" I say. "Why shouldn't I just

blow us all away right now?" I sound crazy, more reckless than I intend to. I wonder if I'm a good actress or if I'm three seconds away from turning the gun on myself. "Like, really. What kind of life awaits us on planet Ursula? But you'd be satisfied anywhere as long as you've still got the Tommys inside you."

"Now Stacey—"

I fire the gun, purposely missing. A neon flash eviscerates the beanbag chair, sending a flurry of Styrofoam pellets into the air.

"I'm only trying to do what's best. I'll do what you kids want. Maybe we should call the Tommys in and take a vote. Planet Ursula is to be founded on democracy, of course."

"Okay, how about you set the destination for Earth." She stands there helplessly, like an unplugged TV set. "No," I change my mind, waving the gun dramatically. "Put it back the way it was. I wanna fly in circles. I command you to do it, so you have to, right?"

Silently she flips some switches, gently strokes a button here and a button there.

Behind me, through the echoes of the corridors, I hear Tommy's voice. "Mom—I mean Ursula, I can't sleep. Can I have some milk and cookies?" The control she has over them—if she appeals to the Tommys for help, I'm doomed.

I aim and pull the trigger. Ursula vanishes in a fluorescent spray of plasma.

XV.

So now what, I think as I stare at the empty space where Ursula stood. An electricity in the air from the zap gun, my tongue feels like it licked a battery.

Tommy leans against the doorframe in his pajamas, sleepy and confused. "Ursula?" he says.

I'll tell him and the other Tommys she was an evil robot overlord programmed for a suicide mission by the giant, sentient microchip that took over the earth. They'll moan and mourn for a while but the vacuum of space will make them soon forget. Then we can go back to the old routine. We'll eat junk food and have sex, huff gasoline till we pass out. We'll play pong, and hopefully one day figure out how to install *Astral Frontier*. When the first of us is old enough, we'll order alcohol from the beverage dispenser, become alcoholics, maybe even get drunk enough once to try an orgy. We'll fall asleep on the toilet and cry under the covers for our lost earthly lives until we forget we ever had them. We'll never grow up. We'll stay the same shallow, selfish people we've always been. But at least that way we'll never learn the truth, about what happened to Earth, about what undoubtedly terrible future awaits us. We'll fly in circles and live this way forever. When we die our bones will float in the dead ship's hull like ghosts.

Wonder Woman's Tampon

I saw her once, in line at a service desk in an overcrowded airport terminal in Orlando. Her invisible plane was in the shop or had shattered into a million glass marbles as she battled an army of cryogenically unfrozen Hitler clones. That's my guess. I thought she herself could fly, like so many of the bright-caped men she associates with, but it could be I'm thinking of another. She rested fingers on her concrete thigh, near where her Lasso of Truth was holstered. Anyone could see she'd use it on the ticket agent. But the line was too long, and some businessman with damp armpits and a comb-over was complaining about the relative leg room of first class. I exchanged looks with her—the ticket agent, I mean. The guy wouldn't have yelled so loud if he were talking to a man.

I heard she's a goddess, or that one of her parents is a god, or that she was sculpted from magic clay and imbued with godhood. Beautiful as Aphrodite, wise as Athena, swifter than Mercury, stronger than Hercules. When she ran two fingers through oil-dark hair, her bracelet clinked against her tiara. I don't know what they're made of—something not of this world, I'd imagine—but the bell tone echoed like a seashell in my ears for days. I wanted to catch her eye, but she's so tall, taller than the pictures make her seem even, that I felt I'd never reach. She gave up on the line and went to check the arrivals and departures monitors, where I was standing. I was this close to her.

When she inhaled, my lungs shriveled. She smelled like earth and salt and candle wax. A little girl on one of those kid-leashes broke free from her mother's grasp, galloped into her and hugged her leg like it was the center of gravity, chapped lips kissing the red leather of her boot. I admit the thought had occurred to me, too. She picked the kid up and cradled her, although she's strong enough that she could have lifted her with one hand or just one finger, and brought her back to her mother. The mother wanted to thank her, get a picture taken or something, but she smiled and declined, tapping her bracelet like a watch.

My flight had begun boarding, but I didn't care. I followed her into the restroom. She grew up on an island of just women, you know. Amazons, they call them. She carried herself gingerly, like someone with a history of apologizing for broken furniture—imagine her gawky teen years: pimples rimming her tiara like jewels, the familiar golden W on a training bra, baby fat softening diamond-sharp cheekbones—but still, people got out of her way, her legs enormous, her steps peremptory. I took the stall next to her. Airport toilets nauseate me, but I had to do it. I sat there on the crinkly paper cover and wondered if what she wore was a one-piece, if she had to strip naked, save for her bracelets and boots, just to go to the bathroom. You think it looks ridiculous, but if you saw her in real life, you wouldn't call it a costume.

Did I mention how tall she is? When she stood, I looked up and she towered over the partition. Eyes downcast, she couldn't help meeting my gaze. Her cheeks reddened, she mouthed "So sorry," and slipped away without washing her hands. I know it's odd of me, but I peeked into the stall she'd been in. She's still not used, I think, to the trappings and conveniences of modern women. She didn't dispose of it in the receptacle. She hadn't even flushed. On her island, they didn't have restroom stalls or dispensers or anything like that. Not even makeup, I'll bet, unless you count mud and flower dyes. What do Amazons have to be embarrassed of? I hit the lever with my foot and let Poseidon wash it into the abyss. Funny to think that even she who strove with goddesses is a woman like you and I.

Habit Patterns

Here is your house, Barbara, its floor plan a mirror image of your neighbor Helen's, as if it were pressed in ink and the lawn folded over like paper, a half duplicated into a whole, like the prints you made in art class. Your room and Helen's meet, nearly touching, in the center crease of the driveway, your parallel windows so close you could walk the gap to Helen's room on a strand of her hair like a tightrope. She never invites you over.

Here is your own mirror image, in the glass above your dresser: your hair oily and tangled, an amoeba-shaped stain on your sweater you fail to hide with that raggedy old scarf. Pimples rim your bottom lip like dribbles of spaghetti sauce. You slept in again and father left without you. You can forget about a ride to school. And you can forget about a shower and a warm breakfast; you're late and haven't the time. Go on, dogtrot to school, try and catch up with the morning bell. It's a race you always lose.

Your black and white world flickers and dims as you hug your books and sprint towards the sound of the morning bell. Someone ought to change the bulb in the projector. But what would it matter? Sloth is sloth no matter how bright the morning.

You're a creature of habit, Barbara. We all are. Unfortunately, not all of your habits are good ones.

✦

Helen is a creature of habit, too. Hers are the correct kind.

She soaks in a bath of milk, rose extract, and honey for two hours each evening. She dresses in silky garments whose opalescence is matched only by the gilded curl of her sun-kissed blonde hair. She smiles politely when addressed, never forgets dates or appointments. No Droopy Dog bags shadow the sparkles in her eyes; it's important for a girl her age to get a good night's rest. Pay attention, Barbara, as you stumble, late and red-faced, into homeroom. See how Helen seats herself in the front row, resting her gloved hands in her lap, nodding attentively to morning roll call. See how the boys look through you and at her, their chins in their hands, moony eyes magnified by their glasses. See how your teacher leans to admire the perfect attendance pin she proudly sports on her collar. His fingers graze her clavicle ever so slightly as he mumbles something about the craftsmanship. Helen is who the boys think about when they lock the bathroom door and don't emerge for what seems like an hour. But you'll have to see our companion film, *Adventures into Manhood*, for more on that topic.

You think about her, too, sometimes, don't you, Barbara? You'd like to run your unwashed fingertips along the ivory of her bare back, to dig your brawny palms into her soft belly and hook your thumb into her navel. You long, for even just a moment, to suck the perfume breath from her moist lips, to chew a clump of her hair like straw.

They're unhealthy thoughts, Barbara. You know that.

Some frames have been cut. Your black and white world jerks and lurches, and now here's the scene: a yellow rectangle of light in Helen's window, your eyes and nose peeking over your windowsill, you watch Helen in the glow of the vanity mirror bulbs. She runs a pearl-handled brush through her hair exactly three hundred times. Her reflection smiles at you, Barbara. That's what you wish. She's only checking for orphaned flecks of lipstick. My, those teeth, morsels of such polish that the Buick in the driveway ought to be jealous.

Hygiene is essential for a growing lady, Barbara, because hygiene and self esteem go hand in hand; they're bosom buddies. But you have no friends, do you? You don't listen. You're always interrupting. The other kids blanch when you talk, so loud, so uncouth. Your hoarse laughter tightens their spines.

Helen is lousy with friends. She's considerate and polite and treats everyone with kindness, even those who don't deserve it, even you. Remember her thirteenth birthday party? She had so charitably invited you. All the kids were there, but you were too shy to talk to anyone. It's a thin line between the timid and the haughty, Barbara. Standing against the wall watching the others enjoy themselves, you needed something to do with your hands, something to look busy with. You cut yourself a piece of the cake, although it wasn't time for that yet. Helen's mother hadn't even put in the candles, and boy was she upset. Then Helen's cousin Tim asked you to dance—you didn't know how—and the idea of it punched you in the stomach and your threw up on the brand new carpet. The mess was the circus color of birthday frosting. Helen was so sweet about it. She dropped a get well soon card in your mail slot the next day.

Now here's Billy, strolling up to Helen's porch with a picnic basket in hand. Watching from the window, dark spots bubble up on your forehead like zits. Is it the green-eyed monster emerging from beneath your acne-scarred face? No, only a brief, fluttering flaw in the celluloid sheen of your black and white world.

Dating is a natural step in the maturation process. It's how young ladies learn to socialize as adults and figure out what qualities they desire in a husband. But what do you know, Barbara? You've never been properly asked on a date. Heaven knows your parents tried, but you remember how that turned out: the leathery smell of the back seat, the hamburger taste of his lips. A nice, college-bound boy, your mother said, the son of one of the community league ladies. It was about time that you got over your shy phase; no matter how clean, how pretty, how sweet smelling you are, if you can't look a boy in the eye or even say hello in a voice that doesn't crack, what good will come of having proper habits? The boy was Tim, from Helen's party, and as he walked you to his car, he muttered, "Oh great, *this* cold fish again." You wanted to prove him wrong, so you drank thirstily from his proffered flask, washing away the sticky popcorn kernels from the drive-in. You were so used to unbecoming dungarees that it was almost a relief when he pulled the hem of the itchy, frilly dress your mother usually only made you wear on Easter. You lifted your arms and conceded without shame, lying still with your eyes closed and breath held, as if you were about to receive a booster shot. As he drove you home, you stared at the side view mirror and pinched pimples, and when he parked in your driveway, you launched out of the car before he even had a chance to request a good night kiss.

And now what, Barbara? Do you feel like a grown-up woman? Of course not. Every weekend you stay in your bedroom reading puerile adventure magazines and playing with children's toys while Helen engages in chaste and rewarding relationships with her peers. Hide against the wall so they don't see you and open your window a thumb's width. Listen to the happy couple's twittering. Billy jokes that he suggested the picnic date just because it's cheaper than the movies. Helen says something poetic about summer's eve and the lengthening days. Maybe she's quoting a famous writer, but how would you know? All you read is that awful pulp.

It's only natural that boys flock to Helen, that all young women look at her admiringly. Goodness thrives on goodness. When Helen splits an apple, she finds a star; you find a worm. Now stifle those tears and swallow all excess saliva. Run to your dust covered mirror and pop your pimples. An ugly habit and a small pleasure, watching the yellow gunk worm out and scraping it under your fingernails, but a pleasure nonetheless.

A boy likes a girl who walks with a spring and not a swagger, so you ought not to gallop like a horse as you follow them on their date, Barbara. Look at Helen: she moves with such poise. At least be casual about it, and stay a block behind. It's all right if you lose them. They're going to the park. You know how to get there.

Now watch from behind those bushes. When a gust of wind hurls the checkered cloth into Billy's face, Helen laughs—melodiously, with delicate fingers pressed to her mouth. A boy likes a girl with a bell in her voice. A little silver one, Barbara, not a cowbell. Billy weighs the cloth down with rocks and Helen sits, brushing her skirt under her legs like a true lady. See how she eats her sandwich, polite little bites. You'd have swallowed it whole.

Beauty is not only physical; it's found in the personality. Billy has such fun just talking to Helen, and he's a perfectly amiable boy. Everyone in your class would agree—everyone but you, Barbara. In kindergarten, before either of you understood the graveness of what transpired, Billy pinned you in the coat room and slid his hand up your skirt, his finger slipping beneath the seam of your underpants. You squirmed out of his grasp and ran back into the classroom, but you weren't upset, only annoyed by his corn-chip breath. Billy's so popular and well-liked today. When you pass him in the hall, he looks at you like it never happened, like he doesn't even know you.

Does it make you angry, Barbara? Do you feel you could cry? Do you feel you don't know what you feel? These are normal teen-age emotions, as illusory as a blown kiss. When you've grown older, you'll look back at the things that are so important to you now and realize how silly they are. What you feel doesn't matter, Barbara. And you ought not to pick the little scabs on your face. You'll only make it worse.

Billy and Helen sure look cross, Helen's tweezed eyebrows knit scornfully. What are they glaring at? It's you, Barbara. You are the dog waste in the green grass of their agreeable spring afternoon. Did you really think they couldn't see you? You're unclean, like a homeless person: dirt and prickly things from the bush on your clothes, blood dotting your face like chickenpox. They must move their picnic elsewhere.

It hurts to be rejected by your peers. Perhaps you'd have greater confidence if you adjusted your habit patterns. Would Helen tear the twitching stems off a daddy long legs like that? No. To relieve stress, she'd relax by herself, perhaps write a poem or paint a picture. And she certainly wouldn't ball her fist and punch herself in the arm until her shoulder went numb, would she?

⏥

Now back at home, you wait and watch for Helen. No one likes a busybody. What your parents must think of you, holed up in your room all the time. If it weren't for school and church, you'd never leave. You'd lie stiffly on your bed and let the grime slowly envelop you. All teen-age girls think hopeless thoughts on occasion, especially during that time of the month. It's perfectly natural to want to disappear and die.

There's Helen and Billy. Listen to the steady creak as they rock together on the porch swing. Peek out the window at them, Barbara, and you'll see the rewards a good date reaps. A farewell kiss is a perfectly acceptable gesture with which a lady expresses affection. It's important to demonstrate to boyfriends that you've had a good time. A little necking may seem like it's only polite, but a true young lady like Helen knows that a *little* necking goes a long way a long way a long way a long way a long way a long way

—⊙—

Something went wrong, the film caught in a loop, but it's fixed now. The clocks of your black and white world continued to tick in the meantime; Billy's left and Helen's gone inside, the porch swing swaying emptily.

Look in the mirror, Barbara, and think about what's wrong with you. It's your habit patterns. They need to change. Clean your face with soap and water every morning and every night. Bathe and wash your hair at least once a week. Brush your teeth three times a day. Be kind to your mother and father. Be more ladylike. Be more like Helen.

Now uncoil the lipstick you've borrowed from your mother's vanity table. The idea of makeup is to improve upon natural beauty. You'll just have to make do.

No, no, no. Lipstick goes on your lips. Look at you scrawling it all over your face like a toddler with a crayon. What's the idea, it's not Halloween. You're not a normal girl, Barbara, but the least you can do is try to look like one. Pinch your arm so hard that it bleeds and let the tears rinse your face. You may as well wipe it off with that sweater. It's already ruined.

How effortless Helen makes it look. When the boys and girls crowd in the hallway at school, it's she who's at the center. Beautiful, charismatic, and a fine student, too. It's an effortless intelligence; she smiles through each exam, her teeth so luminous you can copy her answers in the reflection. And she smells like springtime all year round. Did you remember to apply deodorant this morning, Barbara?

Crawl into bed and lie under the covers until it's dark and you can't hear the nighttime noises of your mother and father. After you're sure they're asleep, you reach into the bureau beside your bed and remove the get well card Helen gave you many years ago. On it is a blue cartoon fish, a word bubble blowing from its lips: "I'll be blue till you're in the pink!" You run your fingers along Helen's signature and touch yourself. It's almost as satisfying as popping a pimple.

Careful not to wake your parents, you rise from bed, open your window and slide out like a burglar. Helen always leaves her window open on nights like this; the fresh air clears her pores. This is not behavior becoming of a young lady, Barbara, but we can't stop you. We've given up, though we'd advise you not to chip a nail as you heave yourself over Helen's window ledge and land with a dull thud on the freshly scrubbed floor. But you won't wake her. She's a regular sleeping beauty.

Stand over her, Barbara, and observe. Try to match your breaths to the rhythm of her hushed, somnolent sighs. You've never been so close before. She looks unexpectedly fragile, like the baby deer in our companion film *The Miracle of Birth*. Her milky skin resembles egg shell. You wonder, could you, with the slightest pressure of your thumb on her forehead, crack her into pieces?

So what will you do now? The film ends soon, Barbara, and your black and white world goes dark. But it won't be over. Everything will start again, next period or next semester, unseen classrooms of adolescent eyes always upon you. You're doomed forever to serve as their bad example, the eternal Goofus to Helen's Gallant. So what do you do?

What you do is reach your quaking fingers out and brush a strand of hair from Helen's apple-red cheek. Your fingertips slide across her skin and she doesn't stir. You discover at the base of her jaw line a tiny, almost unnoticeable yet significant pink zit. Nobody's perfect, Barbara. Does that make you happy?

But you can't hear us anymore. You're transfixed. You caress it like a jewel on a ring, trace the minuscule contours with your finger. You take Helen's chin and gently tilt her head. Biting your lip, you position your pointer fingers on either side of the pimple, take a deep breath, and squeeze.

The Enormous Television Set

The enormous television set stood tall and wide on display at Morgenstein's Discount Electronics Warehouse, its smaller, cheaper brethren flanking it on each side, every set tuned to the same channel, their speakers a soap opera chorus. The synchronized light and sound was beautiful in its way—even as one character called another "A dirty, cheating bitch!" in a sharp, sibilant voice—but the enormous television set, sensing a customer's interested eye, wished to glow brighter, sing louder than the sets around it. It had been in the store for more than a week now and every time a passing gentleman or lady had inquired about it, he or she left the store with a smaller and more affordable model, or nothing at all, despite the salesman's best efforts. "After all, who really needs a TV *that* big?" said one almost-buyer, whose wistful eyes, even as he carted out his new 48-inch model, gazed over the salesman's shoulder at the enormous television set.

☝

It remembered its birth at the factory testing station. Plugged into a three-prong outlet, a simple caressing of the power button, and—click—it surged with life, a tiny white pixel in the center of its glass expanding instantly into a 72-inch square of black and white fuzz: blind, unspeaking, unknowing. And then darkness, shut off and couched in a Styrofoam and cardboard womb, to be reborn in the aisles of Great Deals Electronics and More Superstore, where it was displayed with pride at the end of the aisle, admired by all who passed by. The salesmen there were so good to it, cleaned its screen every day, polished its buttons, adjusted the picture so that its balance of warm and cool colors was just right.

Many people wanted to buy the enormous television set, and many people did. Except that every time someone pointed at it and said, "I'll take that one," he or she went home with not *the* enormous television set but *an* enormous television set, one identical to the real article but still boxed and ignorant, having waited patiently with the others in an austere row beneath the enormous television set's display. The store model pitied them, for they would never know life the way that it did; they spent most of their time alone, surely, their screens cool, black, and lifeless, except during the evenings when their owners were home. Children smudged fingerprints all over them, and careless guests set their highball glasses on top and left ugly rings of condensation. Meanwhile the enormous television set remained pristine and cared-for on its perch in that lovely high-ceilinged building, fluorescent lights casting an ample, flattering glow upon it.

But then one early morning, amid murmurs of "new shipments" and "improved, state-of-the-art models," the enormous television set was lifted by a monstrous forked machine, deposited into the cramped blackness of a shipping crate. After some time and movement, the crate top peeled open, a rush of light revealing the mustachioed faces of two burly, sweating men. They slid the enormous television set out of its box and left it haphazardly on a patch of linoleum floor, which had evidently not known a broom for some time, amongst other TV sets, some that it recognized and some, like a Sylvania 17-inch and an Olevia 32-inch whose base had cracked, which were foreign and ugly, encased in dull, cheap plastic, with foggy glass that even if shined would never glimmer even half as bright as the enormous television set's. This was not good company, and there was certainly nothing super about *this* store.

The salesmen at Morgenstein's were crass and rude and worked on commission. Desperation leaked out of their armpits and stained their shirts a brown-yellow that matched the tint of fingers that pinched cigarettes as they marched to the break room. On Fridays they talked of stopping at McDonald's after work and then going to the liquor store across the street to split a case of Pabst Blue Ribbon, which they undoubtedly drank in the parking lot without shame, whereas the Great Deals salesmen had dined at Chili's and ordered mixed drinks at the bar before going home to their wives, whom they were not divorced from, and their children, for whom they deposited five percent of every paycheck in a college fund. By the end of its first week at Morgenstein's a thin layer of dust had accumulated on the screen of the enormous television set and none of the employees seemed to notice.

Presently the one with the plastic nametag that read SAL patted the enormous television set to demonstrate its sturdiness to a customer and left a palm print on its side, his hand greasy with the oil he used to slick back his hair in an uneven pompadour. It could easily be wiped clean, but no one bothered.

"This," the salesman named Sal was saying, "is the kind of TV that lives with you. It's more of a roommate than an appliance, you know?" He was talking to a shriveled old man in a red baseball cap that matched his suspenders. The old man nodded, eyed the price tag (which made the enormous television set itch on its side and would no doubt leave a sticky residue once removed), and opened his mouth to speak, but Sal went on. "Tell you God's honest truth, uh, what did you say your name was?" The old man said his name was Otto. "Tell you God's honest truth, Otto, this is the very set I got myself, in my very own home. Makes my wife's parties a lot more bearable, I can tell you that much, ha ha. But seriously, this is a great little—big! I mean big. This is a big little machine that's great for company. It's like having a movie theatre in your living room. You look like the kinda guy who likes to entertain. You know, poker night, block parties, whatever, huh, Otto?"

"Uh, no," the old man said, scratching his chin, which hung down his neck in a wrinkly skin-bubble. "My wife is—ah, recently passed."

Sal slapped the old man on the shoulder. "Sorry to hear that, buddy. I wasn't gonna do it, but now I guess you've convinced me. See that price tag right there?" He pointed. "Subtract two-hundred—no, two-fifty—from that number, okay, and it's yours."

"Well," said the old man. He put his hands in his pockets.

Sal reached into his shirt and removed a newspaper insert advertisement from one of Morgenstein's top competitors. "Take a look at this," he said, pointing to a picture of the enormous television set. "You go anywhere else you'll pay nearly double what I can offer. I'm doing you a favor, Otto." Sal waved the insert in the old man's face, holding it carefully so that his thumb covered the part that showed that the ad was dated nearly two years ago.

"Hmm," said the old man. He stared into the enormous television set's vast screen, the flashing lights and bright colors of a game show set. Sal stood, lips pursed; the enormous television set could sense that he was trying to send the old man psychic messages. You will buy this set, you will buy this set, he thought, repeating it like a mantra. The enormous television set did not care for Sal, but it had to agree.

"Okay," said the old man, nodding. "I'll take it."

The man named Otto lived in a two-story house of which the enormous television set had only ever seen two rooms: the foyer, as it was carried in by a group of foul-mouthed moving men who shared private jokes while Otto stood by, fingering his wallet, unsure whether he was obligated to tip, and the living room, perfectly cozy for the enormous television set, apart from the thin, frilly drapes which did little to keep bothersome patches of sunlight off its screen and a great, gaudy grandfather clock that ticked incessantly. However, Otto was otherwise kind to the enormous television set, having connected it to a cord in the wall that made it feel more alive than it had ever been, even more than during its stint at Great Deals. Oh, what a wondrous feeling it was when Otto lay on the couch fingering the remote control, sending the enormous television set through myriad vibrant channels. Sometimes Otto would, absentmindedly or perhaps out of sheer boredom, push the enormous television set past *all* the channels, into the no man's land of black and white static, and a giddy rush would overwhelm it, as if it were getting away with something naughty.

Otto lived alone and liked to leave the enormous television set on even when he wasn't watching it, just to have background noise to keep him company. Yet he did not miss his wife. The enormous television set knew this because Otto often talked to it. Or maybe he was talking to himself and the enormous television set only overheard. "*She* never let me watch this one," he said. "We always had to watch *her* shows." Sometimes he walked around the house in nothing but socks, underwear, and suspenders. "My house," he'd chant, "and I can do whatever I want."

One night, when it was so dark that the only light came from the tiny, red LED at the enormous television set's base, Otto stumbled down the stairs muttering incoherently, collapsed on the couch, and clicked the remote's on button. He seemed to be using the enormous television set more for a source of light than to watch programs, as even with the cable package Otto had, there was nothing but dead air and infomercials on at this hour. Otto traipsed into the kitchen and returned moments later with a long-necked, amber-colored bottle. He took deep swigs from it and choked. He stood up, steadied himself against the coffee table and climbed the stairs on his hands and knees, leaving the enormous television set alone with the empty room and its own azure glow. From upstairs came thuds and clunks and the sharp crash of broken glass. Finally, Otto stumbled back downstairs and rolled onto the couch. He was wearing a simple black dress that must have belonged to his wife, and he sat there alternately sobbing and sniffing the fabric. The enormous television set hummed uncomfortably. After some time, Otto wiped his face, slapped his cheeks, and took a deep breath. An embarrassed calm settled over him, as if he'd suddenly realized someone was watching. Then he clapped his hands on his fuzz-covered knees, heaved himself up, clutched his chest, and fell head-first into the coffee table, shattering the glass top and littering the floor with shards that reflected gleaming fragments of the images on TV.

The enormous television set stayed with the dead man for a long time. After a while his skin turned gray, and the enormous television set was glad that it possessed no sense of smell. It was sick of showing the same channel all the time and wished there were someone around to change it. The days and nights, as well as the TV shows and their reruns, began to blur together, and the enormous television set started to hate the man who'd bought it. It was glad he was dead and only regretted that his passing hadn't come less peacefully.

It missed the company of the other television sets at Morgenstein's, even the salesmen. It missed having its buttons caressed and the small, bright jolt of the remote control's signals. It stood a solitary vigil in the empty house, listening to the faint hum of the central air, the creaking of the wood, the swooshes of cars passing by outside. The enormous television set knew nothing but the world contained in that living room: dead, grey Otto; the old couch with cigarette burns in the left arm; the grandfather clock; the broken coffee table; and a photograph on the wall that the enormous television set spent much of its idle time studying, for its black plastic frame reminded the enormous television set of itself. Pictured was a young family: mom, dad, and a little boy and girl. Mom and the daughter wore plain white dresses and dad and the son wore matching black bowties, so that the photo had the look of an incestuous group wedding. The enormous television set sometimes longed to meet this not altogether photogenic family, and other times it wished the photo would shake loose from the wall and fall facedown on the floor so it would never have to look at it again.

After what seemed an interminable period of isolation, the doorbell rang, and rang, and rang again. And then there was the front door creaking open, and a soft, tentative voice: "Hello? Anyone home?" The enormous television set wished it had fingers with which it could press its own buttons and turn its volume up to the max by way of answer. It couldn't, but someone stepped closer anyway. "Otto? It's Trudy Beedle, your neighbor? I was wondering if you might—" The enormous television set caught only a brief glimpse of Trudy's bottle-red bouffant before the tip of her high heel caught Otto's stiff leg and she ran out of the house screaming.

Surely that was it for the enormous television set. It'd be stuck here alone with Otto's rotting corpse until the power company shut off the electricity and there it would sit in darkness for the rest of its days.

But lo, it wasn't long before two men in gray jumpsuits and with white domes over their mouths and noses came rushing in carrying a large silver tray. They heaved Otto's body into a nylon bag, set him on the tray, gave each other a high five for a job well done, and left the house whistling. Not long after, a bunch of big-armed men paraded in and lifted the enormous television set into the open face of a crate, which they sealed with a machine-like efficiency that jogged memories of its birth at the factory.

It was fascinating, the enormous television set thought as it rocked gently to the steady gallop of an automobile, how many people there were whose job it was to move a thing from one place to another. A short, topsy-turvy trek in the arms of the movers followed, and then a slow, deep sinking, and finally, the stillness of ground. The mouth of the crate dropped open, blinding light flooded in and shone on the surface of its screen, and the four faces from the photograph in Otto's living room hovered over it. The man beamed. The children's mouths were two wide Os. The woman scowled.

She was the first to speak. "I don't know. We've already got a TV, and it's just such a—a monolith."

Immediately the children pouted. The man rubbed the side of the enormous television set affectionately. "Lois," he whined, "it's all Dad left us. It's a memento. I know you never liked him, but—"

"I never *met* him," she said. The children watched her intensely, ready to trigger a temper tantrum. Their father, when their mother wasn't looking, nodded at them encouragingly. The woman silently calculated her options, then threw up her arms in surrender. The children cheered as the man took apart the rest of the crate with a crowbar.

The enormous television set liked its new home very much. The man—Stanley was his name, or at least that's what the woman called him—connected it to a box that sent signals all the way from a satellite in space, which made the enormous television set woozy with unknown feelings, overwhelmed by the blunt shock of the satellite's cosmic rays. It soon became accustomed to it, however. While the children, Bobby and Jane, occasionally shot darts from plastic guns and left circles of moisture on its screen, they also whined and pouted and begged Stanley to purchase for them the latest high-tech video game system, and he did, despite the woman's insistence that it would distract them from their homework. When they played their games it tickled and pinched the enormous television set, but in a rather pleasant way, each pixilated explosion sending tingles throughout its body.

The woman had a name, of course, but the enormous television set preferred not to know it. It did not much care for her, for she was a shrew who was constantly switching the enormous television set off and accusing it of being an energy-sucker. She routinely pulled Stanley away as he was watching sports. The woman was jealous, that much was obvious. Why wouldn't she be, when the enormous television set shone clean and bright on every inch of its surface while she—her hair already graying, skin dry and flaky—was rolling past the edge of her youth at such a pace that the man Stanley often looked over her shoulder at the TV as he talked to her. Sometimes Stanley would creep down in the middle of the night, take an unmarked VHS tape from the back of the cabinet, and play a pornographic movie on mute while he stroked himself under his flannel robe. This turned the enormous television set's hue reddish.

Little Bobby, when he had grown a bit older, once invited a few friends over for a sleepover, and when he was sure his parents and sister were asleep, played the pornographic video. Some of the boys giggled and peeked through their fingers at the screen, as if they were watching a horror film. Others sat with their mouths agape and their hands over their crotches. They all agreed that this was the best sleepover ever and that Bobby was "the man." Then the woman walked in, flicked on the light, and shrieked, "What the hell are you watching?" She snapped her fingers and said, "I want to know who's responsible right now." The boys stared at the floor, a mess of neon sleeping bags and white pillows speckled with Cheeto dust. Bobby turned off the enormous television set. As if on cue, the other boys went into the other room as Bobby followed them with pleading eyes. Just then, as the woman prepared to sit down with Bobby to have a stern talk, Stanley trudged in, his eyes bleary with sleep. "What's going on?" he said in a creaky voice. One glance at Bobby and he knew. The woman said something quietly to him and then turned back to Bobby, nearly hysterical with shame. "No TV, no games, straight home after school, extra chores." Bobby looked past her at his father and with their eyes the man and boy made a deal that no punishment would be enforced by Stanley and no incriminating word would be spoken by Bobby. The next morning, as the woman tossed the video tape in the garbage on her way out to the curb, Stanley looked at the enormous television set and sighed.

The family grew older. The enormous television set remained much the same. Its video game system became boring and out of date, so the children whined and begged until Stanley bought them a new one. The VCR was thrown out, too, replaced by a brand new DVD player. Time moved faster now, for it seemed Stanley was replacing out-of-date video game systems every few months, and it always saddened the enormous television set, just a little, to see the old ones go.

And then there was no need for video games anymore, for Jane had entered high school and grown too old for such toys, and Bobby—well, Bobby wasn't around anymore. The enormous television set never knew what happened, and, it supposed, neither did the family. It had been there the night Bobby didn't come home from school, had watched the policemen trudge in and out of the house in the days that followed, watched the woman serve them coffee and answer their questions while Stanley sat on the couch staring at the TV although he'd evidently forgotten to turn it on and Jane sat on the stairs pouting even more than usual. It had been there with the family as they waited by the phone, pretending to busy themselves with checkbook balancing, knitting, and homework, and it had watched excitedly as they were interviewed by the local news and then proudly displayed them on screen that night at eleven.

Gradually, the enormous television set became used to Bobby's absence. In fact it benefitted from it. Since Bobby had gone away, Stanley kept the enormous television set on almost all the time, even when no one was watching. Stanley and the woman still argued about the energy bill, but it was in a much quieter way than before. Typically the woman would sigh a lot and throw papers at Stanley's chest, and he would simply ignore her and turn the enormous television set's volume gauge higher and higher. Stanley spent most nights on the couch and so the enormous television set never wanted for company. Actually, Bobby's disappearance was the best thing that had ever happened to it.

The enormous television set didn't know the girl Jane very well. She spent most of her time in her bedroom and only watched an hour or two of TV each week, shows about attractive young people in expensive clothes. When Jane got a boyfriend, she and the boy would sit for hours before the enormous television set, although they weren't exactly watching it. The enormous television set followed their relationship with some interest. They sat or lay together on the couch kissing and ran their hands wildly over, then under, each other's clothing. Once he removed his shirt and she did the same, and he buried his head in her breasts and uttered a disturbed sound like weeping. The enormous television set thought it very unnatural. Soon they were "going all the way" (as Jane later described it to a friend over the phone) during *The Tonight Show*. The whole thing didn't last as long as the opening monologue. The boy pulled up his pants, condom still capping his dwindling member like a deflated balloon animal, slid on his shirt, and whispered "I love you" into Jane's ear. She grimaced, then half-smiled—in a mean sort of way, the enormous television set thought—and said, "Just go." That was the last that was seen of Jane's boyfriend.

But there were other boys, a new one almost every weekend, and the same routine: pawing, panting, the boy's embarrassment, and Jane's sendoff. Often Stanley and the woman were home, but they tended to stay in their separate bedrooms (Stanley had moved into the missing boy's at one point, complaining of the couch's ill effect on his back) and showed little interest in the goings-on of their daughter. Jane did not seem to be an altogether happy girl, but she had a certain drive; her sharp eyebrows betrayed a subtle anger, whereas her parents watched the enormous television set with unblinking, dried-up orbs of resignation.

Eventually Jane left, but not in the way that Bobby did, for Stanley and the woman did not box up all of her belongings and they still said her name into the telephone sometimes, sighing and tearing up when they heard the answers to questions such as "Will you make it down for Thanksgiving this year?" and "When can we meet him?"

By this time the enormous television set was not what it used to be. Battling network logos had burned into the bottom corners of its enormous screen. Occasionally the sound would go mute and return so quickly that the enormous television set could only hope no one had noticed. Worse was that it developed a habit of flickering black and white, which caused Stanley to rise from the couch and whack its side with his palm. The enormous television set felt it should be upset by this betrayal, but in truth it was just too tired to feel much of anything.

So it wasn't surprised the day Stanley directed the moving men to mount the very large, very thin flat screen television set on the wall above it. When they were done, Stanley beamed and pressed the power button with a gentleness he had never shown the enormous television set. The new TV shone with a brilliance the enormous television set had never imagined. The difference between it and the new set was immeasurable. "Get a load of that picture, boys," Stanley said, clapping one of the moving men on his back. "So you wanna take this heap off my hands," he said, motioning at the enormous television set.

"It'll cost you," they said. Stanley wrote a check and the men loaded the enormous television set onto a wide, flat wooden cart like a gurney and strapped it in with bungee cords. Just before they wheeled it out of the house forever, the woman emerged from the next room. She offered the moving men some lemonade, which they declined. "Best be on our way, ma'am." And then, with a heretofore unrevealed grace, she ran her hands softly along the sides of the enormous television set and said, "I might actually miss this big old thing. The house looks empty without it."

The enormous television set sat quietly in the junkyard

amongst towers of broken and abandoned electronics. It thought it recognized some of the video game systems from the old days but couldn't be sure. That had been a long time ago. It wasn't so bad here. With no satellite, cable, or broadcast signal, the only way of telling time was the good-morning-good-night cycle of the sun and moon, and after a while even that was inconsequential.

Once, months or years or days—how could it tell?—after it had been deposited there, some teenagers broke into the junkyard at night. They kicked stuff around and smashed random objects with golf clubs, baseball bats, tennis rackets, whatever they could find. One of them jumped on top of the enormous television set, yelled, "Look at me! I'm on TV!" and swung his bat into the screen, shattering it with a force that sent reverberations up the bat and into the boy's hands. He dropped the bat into a pile of old VCRs and ran off giggling to join his friends, who yelled from the other side of the yard that they'd found an old refrigerator, and they needed him to help flip it because one of the boys had agreed on a bet to eat whatever food they might find inside.

With its screen smashed, an empty zigzag shape like a cartoon explosion in its center, the enormous television set saw only darkness. Perhaps, devoid of sight, its intuitive senses increased, for with a flash of insight as bright and overwhelming as a power surge, the enormous television set entered a state of peaceful and absolute consciousness. Unfettered from the facile physical plane, it spread out and became one with everything, from the stars illuminating the outer reaches of the cosmos to the antennae of a single microscopic termite to which the whole of the junkyard was an endless cosmos.

And as its essence floated ever outward and kissed the airwaves of planets in far-away solar systems, it knew this: Bobby was in the junkyard, resting sleeplessly in a makeshift coffin. The coffin was spinning now, bones jumbling together like dozens of dice in a desperate gambler's hands. The enormous television set knew, though it did not care to, by the sound of the teenagers' screams, that they would not easily forget the moment they heaved the refrigerator door open and shone dim, merciful moonlight over Bobby's skeleton.

But it seemed foolish, then, to be so affected by mere objects, nothing more than junk in a junkyard.

The Modern Stone Age

I.

At first they walked the earth with nothing. Their hands clasped no tools, their bloodied knuckles dragged along the treacherous terrain. They dwelled in caves and slept, ate, and mated in these dark, stone wombs, emerging from their maws naked like newborns each morning to scavenge for food. They survived almost by accident, chewing tough weeds the females had foraged, sucking the oily insides of pilfered pterodactyl eggs. On occasions of great fortune, the males stumbled upon an already wounded and dying wildebeest and feasted comfortably on the meat scraps for days, the constant hunger that haunted their lives temporarily mollified. Theirs was an existence bereft of intention. They did not think; they acted. When a male identified a female with whom he desired to mate, he took that female forcefully. And when that female already belonged to another male, on the grounds that he'd grabbed her wrist in his furry palm first, he sent a heavy, flat stone—the first tool—into the other male's skull.

But then came the sharp point of a stone dagger, succeeded shortly by the spear. And finally, glorious fire issued forth from the hot friction of two sticks held by an enterprising female. Nourished in body and mind by the abundance of meat these inventions afforded, they fashioned the first wheel, and with this the most advanced specimens eventually migrated far away from their unwelcoming environs, leaving behind the soft-willed and atavistic Savages, whose hammer-browed visages hid sodden brains incapable of speech or innovation, whose clumsy hands could scarcely wield fists let alone torches and spears. Abandoned, the Savages continued to live, wildly and without meaning, among feral and heartless animals, huddling for warmth in the facile safety of their caves.

Meanwhile, the migrated few ushered in a glorious new epoch. They settled in the flatlands and constructed new contraptions of unnatural complexity and novelty. Now the barren, threatening homeland they had known was but a distant memory as the men steered their wood-and-stone cars along the paved roads of suburban Bedrock and the women vacuumed the floors of their luxurious ranch houses with wheeled baby woolly mammoths. Walking upright and clothed, they regrouped, from loose-knit clans, to neighborhoods and city blocks, to, finally, husband and wife. The men worked civilized jobs that utilized the technological advancements of tamed beasts, while the women kept home with a wide array of state-of-the-art appliances and utilities: the indoor plumbing of a mastodon's trunk, the washer of a pelican's enormous pouch, the sewing machine of a mounted bird's needle-beak. Things had evolved. Life was easier than it had ever been.

II.

But was it any better, Fred wondered as he reclined in the tree hammock in his neat, straight rectangle of a backyard. He downed another beer, the stone can chalking his tongue with an unpleasant aftertaste. To think, he used to slurp water from murky streams. Lately, the comfort had begun to overwhelm him. At work, perched atop the bronto-crane, he'd sometimes be hit in the pit of his stomach with a sudden panic, a fluttering, desperate feeling like he'd swallowed a live bird whole. He'd sit still and methodically tighten and loosen his lizard-skin necktie while his boss Mr. Slate yelled for him to quit slacking. Fred rolled off the hammock and crawled through the yard searching the numerous empties strewn about for any remaining droplets. Odd, he thought, how he spent every day at work riding and co-operating with the same creature that Wilma served to him on a plate for dinner.

Just then, Wilma opened the back door and Dino came tumbling out, yipping and yapping. The poor mutt sniffed the empty cans and licked Fred's chin affectionately.

At one time Fred would've been hurling a spear into Dino's supple flesh as the dinosaur whipped his snakelike neck and brandished bone-crushing teeth. There was something vaguely unnatural about it. Prey had become pet. Dino squatted in the grass and released a putrid turd. Fred fanned the stinking air from his nose and kicked an empty can into Dino's muzzle. He yelped and galloped back inside.

In the next yard over, Barney pushed a dolly with an

alligator strapped to it that clipped blades of grass with its sharp teeth.

In earlier times there was no language, no names. You'd simply introduce yourself by pounding your fist on your chest and grunting. Fred relished the precise movements of his tongue as he beckoned his friend: "Barney boy, Barney, old buddy, old pal, Barney!"

Barney swerved the alligator and met Fred at the other side of the stone fence. "Uh, you called, Fred?"

"Barney my boy, you doing yard work on a Sunday? Cage the gator and take a load off."

Barney leaned his elbow on the fence and rested his chin in his palm. "Like to, Fred, but I told Betty I'd have the lawn done by the time she's back from Stoneworth's."

"So you're done." Fred shrugged. "Don't you know, pal, when the wives're away, the boys will play." He chuckled mischievously.

Barney stared blankly as he thought it over. "If you say so, Fred." He began to climb the fence, his posture betraying the hunched, brutish gait of old.

"Wait a minute. There's a price of admission. How's about you go grab us some beers from the kitchen."

"Sure thing, buddy." Barney disappeared into his house and reappeared a moment later with a six-pack of Rockweiser. He sat recumbent in the shade of the palm tree and handed a cool, sweating can to Fred.

Fred finished the can in one gulp and chucked it over the fence into Barney's yard, where it bounced off the alligator's snout. Irritated, the alligator looked up and sneered. "Betty's at Stoneworth's, you say? Kiss your paycheck goodbye. Women," he spat, "they don't know how good they got it."

III.

Inside, Wilma, on her hands and knees, scrubbed the sandstone floor with a porcupine brush. Working the stain Dino had just left, she clenched too hard—porcupine wincing—and pricked her fingers. She dropped the brush and stood. The porcupine scurried under the sofa. Hot blood slithered down her fingertips. It reminded her of scavenging wild berries, a long time ago. Their palms calloused and juice-smeared after an endless day of combing bushes and fields, often the females would be so tired by evening that they collapsed in a pile at the foot of a nearby cave. Now every couple had their own neat domicile, each house perfectly positioned along its immaculately aligned street like a molar in a T. Rex's gums. Wilma could go a week or more without seeing another woman, even Betty, who lived right next door.

She licked a drop of blood from her finger. She cupped her hands and watched the blood collect in her palm, then wiped it across her rabbit fur tunic, a solid, ruddy streak from the base of the neck to her hip, and wrapped her hand snugly in the fuzz of her skirt to staunch the bleeding.

She looked down at the mess she'd made of her garment and uttered a single syllable: "Ug." Then, her face flushed, she tugged her pebble necklace, cleared her throat and said, "Oh dear." She pattered into the laundry room, let the dress collapse at her bare feet, lifted the washer's beak and dropped it into the soapy water. The pelican that served as washer waggled its eyebrows and grinned, then began to shake its floppy beak vigorously.

Wilma stood naked in the doorframe, gliding her buttocks along the stone wall, as smooth as a woolly mammoth's tusk. She wouldn't put on a new dress, she decided. She would stay this way. Natural, she thought as she thumbed a furry tuft of pubic hair. She let down her bun of hair as a scenario played in her mind: Fred barging in, grabbing her by the neck with his brawny, dirt-caked hands and dragging her outside—out in the open for anyone to see—and taking her there, by force, like in the old days, sticks and rocks scratching her back, her skull knocking against the hard ground.

But it was only a fantasy. They hadn't touched each other in weeks.

IV.

After a couple of trips back to the refrigerator, Barney had had quite a few drinks, but nowhere near as many as Fred. Barney rubbed his back pleasantly along the ridges of the tree and watched the clouds in the sky. Fred had pissed his loincloth and was now mumbling, "What's the big deal? That's the way we used to do it. Piss on the ground, not into the trunk of some animal. Shit where you piss. Eat where you shit. That's nature."

Barney nodded absently. He had no reason to feel

nostalgic for the nature Fred spoke of. He'd been the tribe runt. His meek reflection looked back at him in the riverbed one day as a young male, and from then on he acted in accordance with the smallness he perceived. He hung back during the hunts, letting the alpha-Ug (who later called himself Fred) and the other sinewy, boulder-headed Ugs tousle with the large cats and small dinosaurs whose meat provided precious sustenance. In truth, Barney would have preferred to pick berries with the females, but he knew such a preference was deeply shameful in the tribe. For his cowardliness he always received the least desired cut of meat, stone-tough triceratops tail or stink-haunted, chewy entrails. During mating season, Barney's candidacy went unacknowledged by both the Ugs and the females. He'd watch longingly the females being dragged by their hair into caves or behind bushes, and then retire to his small, secluded grotto to satisfy himself with his own womanly hands. The Modern Stone Age had been kind to Barney. He wouldn't have survived another year or two of the old life. Presently he had a home warmer than any cave, a loyal and dependent woman, and an icebox bountiful with seasoned meat.

"I'm tellin' ya, Barn—" Struggling to sit up, Fred wrestled with the hammock net. After a minute or two his arms collapsed and he lay back down on his stomach and fell asleep.

Barney listened to the crunch of the tires as the car rolled into his driveway and braced himself for the sight of her shopping bags. Relieved when Betty approached from the back door holding only a single dress by its hanger, he drained another can of beer and burped happily. He waved hello and brought the Rockweiser to his lips although the can was empty. He rose, steadying himself against the tree trunk, and met her at the fence.

"Oh, Barney dear, you'll never believe the deal I found at Stoneworth's this afternoon." She paused then, surveying the half-mowed lawn, and frowned. Barney opened his mouth to explain, but she continued, "What a beaut. You like it?" She held up a blue dress made from the hide of an indeterminate animal identical to the one she was wearing. "And it was so affordable, too. Only—"

Instantly Barney calculated how many hours at work the dress had cost him. Like Fred, he was employed by Slate Rock and Gravel Company, though his job was not so glamorous or high-paying as even Fred's. It would've been cheap flattery to call him a middle manager; he was essentially a paper pusher, and although lugging around stone tablets all day had sculpted his arms, Fred still mocked him for performing what he considered women's work; little difference, he said, between scavenging for contracts and scavenging for berries.

Well, at least it was only one dress, he thought. Maybe Betty was finally starting to curb her spending. "It's, uh, it's very nice, honey. Since you only bought one, I s'pose there's no harm in splurging a little."

"Only one? Are you kidding. I've got more boxes inside. There was no passing up these sales."

Barney hooked his finger around his collar. It was one thing he'd never had to worry about before civilization: bills. He'd hate to have to ask Mr. Slate for yet another advance on his paycheck.

Fred stirred in the hammock. Spying Betty, he rose and smiled. "Ah, Betty Rubble, to what do I owe the pleasure?"

Betty cupped her mouth and giggled. "Oh Fred, you charmer." She took a breath. "Anyway, Barney, I hope you'll have the lawn finished by the time I'm done organizing my new things. You do know how important it is for me to have the outside of the house as neat and pretty as the inside."

"Yeah, Barn, don't you know a man has certain responsibilities at home." Fred scratched himself.

"Uh, sure thing," Barney said as he patted Betty on the shoulder, sending her back into the house. As she sashayed across the lawn, taking care to make a show of tripping on patches of uncut grass, Fred eyed her and rested his hand in his crotch.

V.

Betty stood, arms akimbo, unsure of where to begin. Stacks of boxes and bags from the department store surrounded her, piled on the stone slabs of the sofa and coffee table, on the kitchen counter, and crowding the doorways. Perhaps she had gone a little overboard, but it all—just a few inexpensive trifles, really—made her so happy. It was the mess of it she hated. Each thing should have its own place, she felt. The thought of the way she had once lived, the way some still did—dirty and naked, homeless and without possessions, wrapped in raw, blood-stained animal hides, bugs crawling in hair—she shivered and pawed compulsively at the silkiness of her new dress.

Barney complained that she shopped too much. So many things, he said, she would never wear or use, so what was the point? Couldn't he see that shopping *was* the point? She had to have something to occupy her time. Would he rather she pick berries all day? The Flintstones understood how to live. Routinely Betty would watch through the buffalo hide curtains as her neighbors brought home their latest purchases. A certain cat skin rug had caught her eye recently, and she threw a fit until Barney agreed to work overtime to afford it. Still, she'd had to put it on layaway, and the endless wait agonized her. If only Barney'd ask for that raise. But, no, it wasn't in his nature to take initiative, to act without orders, to desire strongly enough or with enough passion to hurt or kill for it. He was a wide-eyed, furless little cub: reliable, predictable, and undoubtedly weak. And Betty always got what she wanted. Most of the time, anyway.

VI.

Fred had an idea, and with the alcohol buzzing like a swarm of bees between his ears, it didn't matter whether it was a good one or a bad one. The beer all gone, he'd sobered up just enough to reach that tenuous state between gleeful overconfidence and easily triggered violence. "Say, Barn." Fred patted Barney on the shoulder. It wasn't a matter of whether or not Barney would go for the idea, only how much Fred would have to tolerate his hemming and hawing before he inevitably agreed.

"Uh, yes, Fred?" Barney was taking a leak on a nearby tree. Finished, he stumbled into the hammock next to Fred, who put his arm around him and squeezed.

"It occurs to me, pal o' mine, that I haven't dipped my club in any woman 'sides Wilma since, well, since B.C.— Before Civilization, ha ha." Barney chuckled. He was clearly drunk. Better at hiding it than Fred, maybe, but drunk enough to be pliable, even more easily given to suggestion than usual, as long as Fred played it right. "How's about we flashback to cave dwellin' times. You follow me?" An image of Betty in that era played in Fred's mind: taut, muscular thighs from crouching in bushes all day; silky black hair, tangled and dry with dirt, sexy in some animal way; firm berry nipples nesting in her soft, white breasts.

Barney swung his legs nervously, rocking the hammock like a swing. "I, uh, I can't say that I do."

Fred brought his face close to Barney's, like a kiss, the stubble on his cheeks scratching his chin, and whispered into his ear, "I'll take yours, and you take mine."

In the horizon, miles away, a volcano colored the sky with harmless blue smoke. A wild pterodactyl screeched its mating call. Fred watched Barney's solid black pupils quiver as the idea settled in his mind. Of course Fred had seen the way he looked at Wilma when she sunbathed in the yard, had noticed he often timed his exits so that he'd graze her body as he passed through the doorway.

Barney turned to Fred, clapped his hands on his knees, and sighed—or maybe it was a laugh. "Er... huh, huh, whatever you say, Fred!"

VII.

The little violet bird perched patiently atop the clock. Most of its life was a slow, monotonous wait, but it was a living nonetheless. Its job was to watch the sky through the bedroom window, to follow the movements of the sun and moon. Once a cycle, when the sun, on its way up, shone a beam precisely in the center crack of the window-sill, the bird pecked its beak emphatically on the clock's bells to wake the snoozing man and lady of the house. Its legs ached from standing still and its wings were attenuated from disuse, but as an appliance it was safe from predators and warm. And the indoor goings-on of the man and lady were not altogether uninteresting.

Presently the lady of the house was sitting on the bed, fingering a new mink scarf and blushing with delight, her soft cheeks the pink of earthworm flesh. Torn up packages from the department store littered the floor. The door in the next room creaked open. The lady wrapped the scarf around her neck. "Barney? I hope you remembered to put the gator back in the cage." No reply. The bird couldn't remember the last time the man of the house didn't respond with a submissive "Yes, dear" when addressed. The lady slung the scarf off her neck like a whip and said, "You *did* finish your chores, didn't you?" She glanced at the clock. The bird tried to look disinterested.

Gruff, unfamiliar laughter carried into the room.

Someone—not the usual man of the house—was standing in the doorframe now, but the bird couldn't get a good angle on him from its position. The lady gasped, her ruby lips trembling, and rose. A big coconut nose preceded the man as he lurched into the room. His bright orange tunic slung over his shoulder, he was naked, his red penis throbbing like a stubbed toe. "Miss me, baby?" he said as he kicked a Stoneworth's box out of the way.

The lady shrieked. "Fred, why—"

The man named Fred grabbed her shoulders with graceless bear-paws and kissed her, teeth clicking, sloppy tongue moistening her chin. She resisted at first, but when he slid his hand up her dress she bit her lip and moaned and began to kiss back. He grabbed her by the bow in her hair and threw her headfirst onto the bed.

The bird wondered if it should sound the alarm, but that was against protocol. She lay there, her breath heavy with anticipation. The man muttered, "I bet you like this," and picked the mink scarf from off the floor.

"Oh, yes," she cried and lifted her dress. The man spanked her with the scarf for a while as she dug her hands into the sheets and gasped. Then he tossed it aside and swung his head back, his eyes meeting those of the bird upon the clock. The bird remained very still, even stiller than usual, as if a predator had crossed its path in the wilderness.

The man turned sharply back and climbed onto the bed, his stocky, apelike body damp with sweat. He mounted the lady and repeated, "You like this," in time with his movements. His words devolved to animal grunts, his monkey lips peeling back in satisfaction. Finally, reaching climax, he arched his back and pounded his chest, a primeval battle cry erupting from his diaphragm: "Yabba Dabba Doo!"

VIII.

Betty was the only woman Barney had ever been with. They'd met shortly after the invention of cars. A few primitive stone edifices had been erected in what would one day be the center of Bedrock, but life was still a long way from modern. A workable language hadn't emerged yet. Most still went around slapping their chests and going, "Ug! Ug!" Actually, the car had been Barney's creation—just four wheels and a simple rectangular structure of logs—but of course another Ug took credit for it. Yet Barney was the first to have one of his own, and on his debut drive through the encampment, rollicking along the twig-strewn ground (it would be quite a while before paved roads were invented), all the Ugs shook their heads and stomped the dirt enviously while the females appeared from out of their huts and swarmed the majestic new vehicle. Of all the females who called to Barney that day wanting to be the first of her sex to ride in the car, none was more desirable than Betty. The other females were so desperate, shaking their fists with threat of violence or lifting their furry tunics pleadingly. Not Betty. She stood behind the pack, an indifferent smirk on her face. "Ug," she said and pointed, like she knew Barney had no option but to choose her. And she was right. His first time was in that car, and many times afterward.

Now, Barney thought as he approached the Flintstones' house, he could scarcely remember the last time he and Betty had even kissed. She was more interested in shopping than mating. They slept on separate sides of the bed and barely touched. Barney entered the house. His hands shivered with desire and shame as he crept through the door. He followed Wilma's scent toward the laundry room, skulking silently like a burglar. He passed Dino resting on the sofa and then he saw her, framed by the doorway. She was naked, glistening with sweat, as if she expected him. Had she and Fred planned this together? Did Betty know, too? Once again he felt like the runt of the pack, the last to know, the last to grow up.

Their eyes met. Without a word, Wilma waved to him, then reached behind and untied her necklace, let the pebbles roll onto the floor like marbles. Barney blew out the torch on the wall and darkness enveloped them. Fumbling in the dim moonlight, his body bumped hers as his feet grazed the soft cat skin rug. He kissed the peach fuzz on her neck, then stopped himself. "Gee, Wilma, I'm sorry." She put her hand on his mouth and pulled him down onto the rug. He kneeled before her and she pinned his face between her thighs, hairs bristling Barney's cheeks. Her legs weren't smooth like Betty's, but he liked the overgrownness of her. It marked her as untamed somehow.

She pulled him up by his cowlick. When he hesitated, she pushed him onto his back, his head hitting the hard floor with a thud, and clasped his wrists in her hands.

She pinned him, and he lay there helpless and delirious. Oblivious, Dino snored hot breath on the sofa above.

IX.

The kid on his bike tossed the newspaper with such force that the stone tablet frisbeed into Fred's nose and knocked him on his ass. And like always, the delivery boy pedaled away before Fred could smack him. He carried the paper inside and set it on the kitchen table. He sipped his coffee and found it had already gone cold. "Wilma," he called. She took the cup and set it before a tiny fire-breathing dinosaur that warmed it with its flame, then set it back on the table, humming all the while.

Fred glanced at the paper. "What put you in such a mood?"

"Oh, nothing," she trilled, fingering her bare neck.

"Where's your necklace?" Fred asked, too-hot coffee dribbling down his chin. "That was an anniversary gift, you know."

"Must've misplaced it," Wilma said, and skittered into the bedroom.

Her good mood annoyed Fred. An unwanted thought entered his mind and he shook it out angrily. No, of course not, there was no way that imbecile Barney was a better mater than he was. His flesh-club was no bigger than a twig, the puny thing. And as for *his* woman, Fred had shown Betty what it was to know a true alpha-Ug.

The crime column, neatly chiseled into the corner of

the *Daily Slate*, reported that a Savage had wandered into Bedrock city limits and beaten a local man to death with his bare hands. Unconfirmed witnesses were on record claiming the beast had cut the victim open with a sharp rock and run off with his liver, possibly for cannibalistic purposes. An artist's rendering of the culprit—rippled forehead and bulging eyes—accompanied the story.

Fred threw the paper down in disgust. To think, he might've admired those Savages for their tenacity for survival and their simple, unencumbered lives. He spat. They were dumb animals like any other, and weak, too. Things like that, he thought, ought to either be serving people like me or exterminated. Why the authorities allowed those unevolved, dung-smelling freaks to continue to exist was beyond him. Those troglodytes had graduated to little daggers, maybe, but their peanut brains would never comprehend the intricacies of a simple wheel. Everything was fine as long as they stuck to their turf and the civilized people to theirs. Problem was those damn Savages were too dumb to find their way out of their own caves, let alone trying to prevent them from dragging their knuckles into Bedrock. Why, if Fred caught one of them on his property, he'd skewer it and feed the mangy thing to Dino.

But anyway, Fred had more important things to worry about, like getting Betty alone again.

X.

Through the night, Betty cooing by his side, Barney lay

awake and replayed in his mind what he and Wilma had done, revising the course of events slightly each time to suit the obscure triumph throbbing in his heart. As the moonlight reflected in the clock bird's eyes turned to yawning early sunbeams, Barney recollected that it was he who suggested the swap in the first place, he who had stripped Wilma of her clothes and pinned her to the cat skin rug, and he who, as Barney and Fred met at the fence in the yard on their ways back to their respective homes, brushed shoulders with Fred, nearly knocking him flat on the grass, a smug and satisfied smile on his face as Fred skulked away.

In the morning he scooped cereal into his mouth while Betty sat at the other end of the table and prattled on the way she always did. Barney did not bother to affirm her with a "yes, dear," or even an encouraging grunt. He was through playing the obedient and uxorious mate. He thought again of Wilma and became ravenous with hunger. He poured more cereal, set aside his spoon, and slurped straight from the bowl.

Betty waved her manicured hand in Barney's face. "Barney? Are you even listening?" He shrugged, continued to gulp down sweet dino-milk. "I *was saying*, I'll need the Rhinos Club card this afternoon. Stoneworth's is having another sale, and if I don't charge it, I'll have to put it on layaway, and you know how I hate to—"

Barney shot up and hurled his empty bowl against the wall. Betty remained upright, shoulders relaxed, too surprised to cower. "Uh, I've had about enough of you throwin' away all my hard-earned dough on this shit," he yelled, a cocoa pebble stuck to his lip, "No more!" Angry blood surged through him; it was turning him on. He sat down and crossed his legs.

"All right," Betty said meekly, an echo of a sob in her throat.

"Uh, and another thing. You *are* gonna go to Stoneworth's, to take back the garbage you bought yesterday."

Betty nodded and, pouting, went into the bedroom to pack up her returns. Barney helped himself to more pebbles. He deserved it. He felt young and victorious, as if he'd speared his first wildebeest. He wanted to celebrate— with Wilma—but he'd have to wait until tonight.

XI.

As they drove to Stoneworth's that afternoon, Betty recounted Barney's tantrum to Wilma. In the gleaming, tropical sunlight the incident took on a humorous tone, and she found herself less and less bothered by it. Of course, it certainly helped that she had borrowed Barney's Rhinos Club from the dresser when he wasn't looking. "It's not like him to lose his temper," she said.

Wilma fingered her necklace thoughtfully. She'd been quiet since she'd gotten in the car. "Sounds like something's got him hot and bothered," she said.

Betty braked at the intersection, lifted her sunglasses and glanced at Wilma. Was it possible she had found out about Fred? The monkey on the perch dropped the red sign and held up the green. Betty proceeded with a sharp left turn. She would take the scenic route today. Normally she enjoyed a leisurely drive through the suburbs, admiring the order of it all—the perfect green squares of the lawns, the immaculate asphalt of the roads, the precise geometry of the architecture—but she found herself craving sights of a less cultivated nature. "But I guess you must know from barbaric behavior," Betty continued, "what with being with Fred all these years."

"Mm." Wilma gazed out the window.

The rough terrain of the unpaved road scraped Betty's feet. She slowed the car to a gingerly trot. Out here the wild grass grew long and thick, with no regard to aesthetics. It reminded Betty of a man's chest hair. "I mean," she said as though she'd rehearsed it and couldn't stop herself now, "that man can hardly suppress himself sometimes." In truth, she'd found herself getting damp in the loincloth as Barney raged at her. He'd never acted like that before, so much—well, so much like Fred.

Wilma turned and stared at Betty, her line of sight a spearhead on Betty's cheek. "Not like Barney."

Betty nodded, picking up speed now. Chiseled stone signs warned of stegosaurus crossings. They weren't that far out—posh summer cabins dotted the road—but suddenly the land seemed positively feral.

"Would you look at that," Wilma pointed. In the distance, a man crouched in a brook that was hardly more than a mud puddle compared to the neighborhood swimming pool. He cupped water in his hands and splashed his firm pectoral muscles. He was naked but without embarrassment.

Of course, Betty thought. It wasn't a man at all, but a male Savage who'd evidently lost his way. Seeing the car, he jumped out of the water and began to gallop closer. He didn't drag his fists like the caricatures in the *Daily Slate* cartoons, but rather used them like an extra pair of feet. Lupine, he rested on haunches a few yards from the road, his eyes focused and steady.

Wilma grabbed Betty's shoulder and squeezed. She was nervous, but Betty wasn't. Looking into his small, doleful eyes, almost an afterthought to his enormous forehead, something turned in her and she no longer cared about ever making it to Stoneworth's. It wasn't as if all this stuff she'd bought, all the stuff she was going to buy, meant anything, had made her feel halfway as euphoric as she had last night. Why cover herself with gilded clothes when passion required none?

The Savage darted away, disappearing into the woods. Wilma relaxed her grip. The road curved and became smooth again and miraculously, almost instantly, they arrived in Bedrock's shopping district.

"Thank goodness," Wilma said as Betty pulled into the parking lot. "I thought you wanted to go to the store, not the zoo."

XII.

The T. Rex t-bone sizzled over the flames of the hot stove. Wilma jerked the pan and flipped the meat. A little hot oil splashed on her wrists but she didn't wince. With all the cooking she had to do for Fred, she was used to it by now. One side of the steak was overdone. Fred was so finicky about his food. He'd pitch a fit if she served it to him like this. It was hard to believe he'd once eaten raw, bleeding flesh from animals whose hearts hadn't yet ceased beating. Wilma put the ruined steak on a plate and set it aside for Dino, then got another from the freezer and dropped it on the pan, making sure to push the button on the stove that pinched the fire-breathing dinosaur inside the oven, causing it to reduce the heat of its flame.

She'd been distracted all day, for obvious reasons. And also she couldn't stop thinking about the Savage she and Betty had seen. Rumors, lurid tales of packs of Savages breaking into suburban houses at night and raping and killing anything that moved, traveled by telephone horn from one house to the next. Wilma didn't believe them, really, but she had been just a little scared to see one in the wild. It looked threatening, sure, but so simpleminded, too. She wanted to catch it and tame it, keep it like a pet or a servant, use it for her own pleasure.

Wilma flipped the steak. It was perfect, just the way Fred liked it. In the next room he pounded his fists on the table and yelled, "Dinner, woman! Where is it?" Wilma ignored him, transfixed by the sizzling meat. "Damn it, woman," Fred called, "if I don't get my supper now, I'm going to, to, to—well, you don't even wanna know what I'll do."

Wilma plopped the steak onto a plate. She just needed to get Fred out of the house. She lifted the heavy pan, imagined the cracking sound it'd make colliding with his thick skull, then set it back down.

When Betty had dropped her off at home after shopping, Barney had been in the yard, trimming the hedges with a sharp-beaked bird. He gave a little wave, a double wink like something had caught in his eye. A signal, Wilma thought, that he'd meet her tonight. She'd already begun planning what she was going to do to him. It involved a granite pestle.

How silly it was to think that she'd once thought she wanted to be dragged by the hair. What she really wanted was to be the one doing the dragging.

XIII.

Barney, cards in hand, sat across the table from Betty, Fred and Wilma flanking him. It was bridge night, a Flintstone-Rubble tradition, but no one was paying attention to the game, least of all Barney. He'd used to enjoy it, but it seemed to him now too tame, too restricted by exacting rules, too civilized. There was also the matter of Wilma's hand on his crotch. Fred wouldn't notice; he was too busy refilling Betty's coconut cup with booze, leaning close and brushing his arm against her breasts as he poured, acting drunker than he really was.

"I, uh, I guess we should start the game," Barney said.

They had, by this time, been swapping wives for weeks, passing each other at the fence separating their backyards nightly. It was as much of a routine as clocking in and out at Mr. Slate's. If the women knew what their husbands were up to, they didn't show it and they didn't care.

"Whose turn is it?" Fred asked.

Betty and Wilma looked at each other and shrugged.

"Don't know."

"No idea."

They'd been holding the same cards for over half an hour now and no one had bothered to get the game started. Barney wasn't especially eager to. The animal urge to mate ballooned in his lap and he wanted to lift Wilma onto the table.

Fred was playfully hooking his finger under the strap of Betty's dress and pulling it down. Betty giggled, readjusted it, and Fred pulled on it again. Barney turned to Wilma. Unbothered, she smiled, set her cards down and began to massage Barney under the table with both hands. Barney's eye met Fred's. Nobody said anything for a long moment. They set the cards on the table. Betty had never even picked hers up when they were dealt. Wilma ran her arm across the table, still keeping one hand in Barney's lap, and swept the cards onto the floor. Betty made no attempt to fix her loose strap, and Fred had snaked his hand over and was working on the other one. She stared straight ahead, watching for, Barney thought, his reaction. Wilma grabbed his wrist and set his hand in her lap. She was not wearing a loincloth.

Of course they knew, Barney thought. How could they not?

Fred and Betty's seats were empty. Fred had Betty on the floor. He was grunting and peeling off her dress with his teeth; it looked like he was skinning a carcass. Wilma eyed Barney expectantly. He stood, his erection tenting his loincloth, lifted Wilma and set her on the table. As he pulled off his clothes, however, she kicked him swiftly in the chest, hurtling him over the chair and onto the ground. She leapt off the tabletop and mounted him, growling with passion, and he tore off her dress, splitting it in half with his bare hands.

XIV.

The alarm clock bird, who had been recently promoted to the grandfather clock, peeked through the eyehole of its new home and shook its head disdainfully. It had been anticipating the bridge game with some interest, glad finally to have something to look at besides the empty den, besides the big-nosed man named Fred and the lady of the house, Betty, mating in the most unnatural positions.

But now this—it was enough to make the bird molt. These creatures—who possessed the incredible ego to call themselves people, who wore a façade of civilized manners but only until the lights went out, who adorned themselves with cumbersome and useless accoutrements, who mowed their lawns and drove their cars as if it kept the natural world in order, who celebrated the convenience of modern appliances at the expense of the animals they enslaved—these creatures were rolling naked together on the ground like grumbling beasts in heat. No shame, no regard for who might have to watch. Just what did they live in these houses for? Why did they even bother to drape cured animal hides over their bodies and communicate in a needlessly complex language? The bird in the grandfather clock was sick of watching these animals fight against nature. They were no better than brontos that tried to walk on only their hind legs.

The coconut-nosed man, Fred, finished with the lady of the house and threw her aside. She collapsed at the foot of the sofa, flushed and sleepy, her black hair sticking with sweat to her forehead. The man of the house, Barney, had the red-haired lady called Wilma against the wall and was still eagerly going at her. He looked pathetic, like a desperate wolf humping a felled tree.

Fred, apparently wanting his turn with the red-haired lady, hit Barney on the arm and said, "Barn—UG!"

Wilma, clawing the floor, shook her head. Barney, not even slowing down, said, "Ug! Ug!" and hit him back.

The little bird shifted uncomfortably. It should have been gliding across the treetops or digging its claws through the dirt, not trapped in a dim, little box studying the mating habits of loutish Neanderthals.

Frowning, Fred rubbed his irritated arm and steadied himself. With a particularly guttural "Ug!" he knocked Barney with his shoulder so that he fell out of Wilma and landed squarely on his butt, tumescence wagging in his lap.

Betty stood up. "Fred, cut it out, will ya? Leave Wilma alone."

But the one called Fred was already on top of the one called Wilma, chanting, "Yabba dabba doo, yabba dabba doo, yabba DABBA DOO!"

Barney stood and, growling like a saber-toothed beast,

tackled Fred. The women screamed as the men scuffled, biting, pounding their fists, scratching as though their soft ape hands were claws. Finally, Barney pushed himself off Fred, grabbed the club of an unlit torch from the wall and brought the thick end fiercely into the brute's skull. Fred hit the floor lifelessly, deep red fluid spilling from the wound.

Barney dropped the club and looked to the women, who trembled on the sofa. He opened his mouth, but the words wouldn't come. Instead he shouted, "Ug! Ug! UG!" and swung his arms around like a monkey. He'd devolved.

More like a return to his roots, the bird thought, a cheap pantomime of true savagery. Animals didn't mourn, didn't feel regret. Even the stupidest beasts on earth didn't kill their own kind for reasons such as this.

The bird would have no more of man's order. It burst from the clock face but did not announce the time with a melodic cuckoo-cuckoo. Instead it squawked wildly, its wings unsteady, and soared out of the house and upward into the sky. From on high it watched the other animals follow. Its fellow birds from the other clocks and appliances swarmed the clouds. The alligator wiggled out of its dolly. The fire-breather from inside the stove stomped down the road with its cub from the coffeemaker, torching any vehicles that got in their way. The woolly mammoth that had provided running water galloped away, the earth shaking under its giant feet. Even domesticated Dino chewed free of his leash and followed the direction of the herd, the little violet bird pointing the way with its beak. It would lead them to Savage territory and beyond, far from the houses and roads and carefully manicured lawns. And if the Savages caught them or the elements killed them, at least they'd die natural deaths.

Defunct Girl Gangs of North American Drive-Ins

The Zip-Gun Angels. Most active in the years 1954-1958, known among girl gang connoisseurs and anthropologists as the Second Switchblade Era. Over men's undershirts they wore black pirate's eye patches, capping their left breasts like a wink. Other identifiable traits: green eyeliner, unbrushed smiles, chewing sticks of stale bubblegum until strands of glucose threaded their teeth. Activities included the standard girl gang crimes, with a notable penchant for aggression toward babies and the elderly. Picture prams careening down stairwells, tiny soft hands reaching emptily for snatched lollipops. Imagine the sound rutabagas make when they're dumped from rain-drenched grocery bags, landing like fists on the backs of old ladies crumpled on the sidewalk. No known boyfriends, a possibly Sapphic clan. Leader "Dirty" Debbie Dewitt killed by rival Kittens with Whips member in November 1957, a deep scratch drawn in her neck with a knife-sharp false nail coated in poison polymer. The gang dissolved like polish in acetone shortly thereafter.

Dead Dolls. 1964-unknown. Phantasmal or similarly paranormal. Famous for initiation by death and accompanying ceremonies. In dirt-caked drive-in playgrounds they wrapped the initiate's wrists in swing set chains. In their quick, spectral hands a single pine needle became a dagger. The initiate's insides drained until her last breath blew out like a baby's spit bubble. Flimsy and transparent in form; to a distant eye, they were only sheets on a laundry line. Not especially violent, excepting the voluntary initiations. Teasers and voyeurs, they were known to appear in the rear view mirrors and window reflections of teenage lovers' cars. The most common cause of film projector malfunctions in the state of Maryland in 1967, they carried a smell of dust and burning celluloid. Echoes of their onanistic moans can still be heard in the static in the audio systems of the few drive-ins remaining.

Swingin' Sassmouths. 1955-1956. Playing cards sputtered in the spokes of their bicycle wheels, always a queen of hearts. In alleys they chalked their initials on pristine brick walls. They knocked candy jars from drug store counters, snatching handfuls of gumdrops and bits of jagged glass that sharpened their throats and made them cough blood, sweet red venom sprayed on the sidewalk in hopscotch patterns. Filched their older brothers' nudist magazines and studied them in the moon-like glow of the movie screen, ringing the swing set as if playing a game of duck duck goose. When other kids wandered into the playground, they pushed them from the tops of slides and kicked sand in their eyes. Entire gang was killed when a drunken greyhound bus driver barreled into their parade of bikes one dark night in late 1956. When the coroner examined their bodies, he found uniform burn scars over their left hips, the shape of a lipstick kiss.

＊

Ballsy Falsies. 1958-1976. A small, nomadic hermaphrodite gang. Mostly stuck to the eastern seaboard, working carnival sideshows in the evenings and dealing dope to teenagers in the black early morning hours of the third feature. In high heels they had to lean on the speakers for balance as they knocked on the foggy windows of Coupe de Villes and dropped tightly rolled joints through the hot-breathing cracks. When they went beyond the confines of the fairground they often tucked their beards into trench coats, a rare show of modesty from those whose day jobs entailed buzzing lights, spread legs, lifted skirts; in the popcorn-chewing crowds, the men went goggle-eyed, and the women cupped their mouths and fainted. The gang all but disintegrated following the 1976 departure of leader Lance Lady, who became a prominent performer in New York City's nascent punk scene.

＊

Kittens with Whips. 1957-1966. A bite from the frayed end of a kitten's whip, the taste of leather and blood, pinstripe scars birdcaging the victim's face, screams of the dying and already dead: mere trophies of this gang's extraordinary brutality. They waited in alleys, luring high schoolers in long, prim skirts who shielded their sex with textbooks. They smoked firecrackers like cigarettes and dug jagged teeth into white virginal flesh. Priests crossed the street and themselves as the kittens yelled come-ons and peeled off their stockings. Finally, the parents of a girl they'd roughed into unmarriable putty called the authorities. The police trailed the Kittens to an abandoned drive-in, shot at them when they refused to set down the whips they bundled and cradled in their arms like babies. They giggled and caught the bullets in baseball mitt chests, then tied their weapons together and skipped rope. The police fired till their guns clicked emptily. They went back to the station and signed letters of resignation, returned to the drive-in in civilian clothes and proposed marriage. The Kittens accepted, the gang broke up, moved into split level homes, and nine months later gave birth to ten-foot rattlesnakes. In shame their husbands hanged themselves with the whips they'd kept as mementos. The widows wore black the rest of their lives and only left the house to walk the leashed snakes like dogs along bright suburban sidewalks.

The Old Maids. 1960-1963. Nearly every young girl wishes she were older but these girls whitened their hair with peroxide and glue, tattooed wrinkles on their faces that cobwebbed whenever they smiled, which was never, and whenever they scowled, which was often. They wore housecoats like capes and walked barefoot on the nighttime sidewalk till the bottoms of their feet were blacker than the feral cats that nursed on their empty breasts. At the drive-in they buried the window speakers in dirt and watched the films in silence. They resented talkies and Technicolor and space age 3-D glasses. The present terrified them. They crawled into the past and never returned.

Mothers' Other Daughters. 1963-1963. For Hallow-een all the girls in a forgotten town went dressed as one another. They borrowed dresses and imitated hairstyles and exchanged record collections the week before to help get into character. After trick or treating, pillowcases stuffed fat with candy, they returned home, none realizing that she'd gone to her costume's house. In fact, each forgot she was even wearing a costume. The parents were no help; the fathers could hardly remember their daughters' birthdays let alone pick them out of a line-up, and the mothers only sighed, upset that they were late for dinner and the roast had gone cold. The daughters climbed out of their bedroom windows that night and met at the drive-in after the last show, when all the cars were gone. The sliver of the sun marked the horizon like a radioactive toenail. Their meticulous hairdos forming a vast sheet that roiled with their movement, each looked for her true self in the throng of her costumed companions. Recognition failed them, so they lay down on the tire-tread imprints and caked themselves in mud. By morning they'd grown into speaker posts, in rows like tombstones.

The Jailbirds. 1955-1968. Shellac-stiff bouffants helmeted their heads; bullets crushed flat against them like flies on a windshield. Bats nested in their hair, great swarms that carried them from drive-in to drive-in. A man who was getting fresh once ran his hand into one of their beehives and it became lost like in an ACME portable hole from the pre-movie cartoon. Their hair grew taller and taller—skyscraper high. They tied hairspray bottles to the bats' legs and sent them into the thin air for touchups. Eventually their hair grew so heavy that each of their steps forced them deeper into the ground. They sank into the center of the earth and melted.

*

Hellcats in Hot Pants. 1950-1960. Also known as Los Gatos. Concentrated along the Texas-Mexico border, although satellite groups were known to flourish as far north as Oklahoma City. In your grandmother's attic, silverfish glint like coins in the sunlight atop a locked steamer trunk. If you could open it, which you can't, you'd find a pair of threadbare shorts, a railroad spike ruddy with blood crust, and a stack of photos: young women with long, sepiatoned legs, bruised cheeks and blood for lipstick. In one, the lines on the wall precisely measure their height; a short, lithe girl in the center has your grandmother's pale eyes and an ugly sneer. Floorboards below, you sit in her tearoom and pluck a blue hair out of a trail mix cookie. If you found the key your grandmother hides under the sugar jar you might understand why you terrified your boyfriend the first time, carving crimson zippers in the supple flesh of his back, why you tear the hair of the girls who make faces at you as they walk down the hallway at school and whisper "slut" in the lunch line. It's not just you. It's in your blood.

Express Lane

MONDAY

You must be the new girl. I can tell 'cause of that green look about you. Don't worry, I won't run you too hard. So long as you got all the PLU numbers memorized. You *do* have them memorized, don't you? Just kidding, hon. You wouldn't need to know that. You're only my bagger. Work hard enough, though, and we'll have you on the register before you know it. We'll get along fine. It's a great place to work, and oh, you'll just love it here, I promise.

The boy who used to bag, now he was a character. Stuck all the produce stickers to his vest so he'd never have to run over for a price check. Can you believe it?

Kinda shy, aren't you? Well don't worry—I do enough talking for both of us. Because there's one thing about this job you gotta know. And I'll tell you.

Am I Store-Mart's best employee? That's not for me to say—though I have been Employee of the Month more than a few times. I'll be the first to admit I'm not the fastest change-counter. And the PLUs, forget about it, now that we got all these cockamamie hybrids: tangelos, minneolas, grapples, snozzberries, whatever. And I'm a bit of a clumsy bagger, to boot. I'm sure even *you* could teach me a thing or two. But I am pretty good with the register and there's something else I got, too.

What I'm talking about is friendliness. I think it's my duty—*our* duty—to do right by the customer. Let's not even call them that. It's so impersonal. Let's call them what they are, huh? People. Like you and me, like anybody—from the richest, smartest king to the lowliest, noble bum out by the automatic doors, begging for change. (Don't give him any, by the way. He'll only buy booze.) Golly, even Christ Our Savior was born of a modest mortal's womb.

Here at Big Al's Store-Mart we serve people. People who trust us to provide their families with high quality, inexpensive foodstuffs. Nobody likes to wait in line, wasting precious hours of the day, standing there while we scan each and every purchase, as if we don't trust them to pay for it all. So if we can make that unpleasant few minutes all the more less unpleasant—heck, *happy*—then let's do it. Agreed?

Personable! That's the word I was looking for. It's perfect: "person" and "able" together. For I am someone who en*ables* *persons* to feel brighter. Not that I'm bragging. I have a natural intuition about these things. I'm a "people" person and I thank God that He made me this way. It's just a shame He didn't bless some of Store-Mart's other employees—who shall remain nameless—with such a disposition.

Anybody can ask how-are-you, but it takes something else to say it in a way that means you're really interested in the answer and not just expecting a plain old "fine." If that's the best we can do, then bring on those impersonal self-checkout robots, because what's the difference? I mean, who am *I* to tell *you* to tell me you're fine. Maybe you're not fine. Well, then let me know, and I'll do my best to understand—without, of course, overstepping professional bounds. You know the difference between sympathy and empathy, dear? I looked it up. Sympathy is feeling sorry for that poor loser; to engage in empathy is to truly share that which your fellow human being is going through.

Since I was just a girl I always thought that maybe I was suited to be a counselor of some sort. Took some social work classes, even, but—but life had other plans for ol' Delores. And you'll hear no complaints from me. I'm so lucky. I've got this wonderful job, and friends like you, dear, and my "kids" waiting for me at home. What's to want for?

Oh, I wonder sometimes what might've been, out there using my gifts for people who really need it. Ah, but such is life. We can't all wait around for a burning bush to tell us what to do. Because anyway, we've got Fire Codes to worry about, ha ha!

Another thing you should know if we're gonna be working together is that I say and do the kookiest things just for a smile. My coffee mug in the break room has a picture of Mr. Peanut and it says, "I'm a real nut!" Well I'll tell you what, sometimes I think that mug says it all! Get me in the right mood and I'll just do a whole routine on this vegetable or that—never in a lewd way. I get going and pretty soon everyone in line will be howling with laughter and I'll realize I just scanned the same soup can ten times. Whoops!

Like, "Purple cauliflower? Now I've seen everything! What's next, green oranges? Just doesn't make sense!"

Or, "Food stamps? Ever try to mail a letter with one of these?"

I can be a real hoot.

But not everyone wants a joke. You've got to read people. Some maybe don't even seem to want to look you in the eye, let alone have a nice chat. They had a bad day or they're plain grumpy. You think I just grab their cash and scoot them on out of here? No, ma'am. They're the ones that need us the most, and good for them that they chose express lane four, right?

Listen, the trick is to relate. Ask them where they bought their coat or compliment their custom clown checks, for instance. Study them. If you're familiar with the address on the check, recommend a good Italian place nearby. Watch for which tabloid headlines their eyes fix on. Try "What's she gotten herself into now?" or "If I were that rich, I'd get plastic surgery too!"

Is it any wonder I got regulars, people who always go to my line even when there's plenty of checkouts open? Sure, I'll let it slide when they've got sixteen or seventeen items. When it comes down to it, I put people before rules. Rules be darned.

And here's a regular now—Mr. Defranco, how the heck are you?

Mr. Defranco is the fourth grade teacher down at Jefferson Elementary, don't you know. And I'm sure all his students love him. Isn't that right, Mr. Defranco? Say, have you met the latest addition to the Store-Mart family? Say hello to—oh—oh, my poor memory. What did you say your name was?

TUESDAY

You really ought not to let that beautiful hair of yours hang down over your nametag, hon. Don't you want to introduce yourself to the world? You're such a cute little sweetheart and I'm sure there's plenty of folks who love you. So would it kill you to smile more? Like I was saying yesterday—

Oh dear, that reminds me. After your shift ended, in came a lady who really had nothing to smile about. It just breaks my heart to think of it. She seemed like a real nice person, just down on her luck, is all. Why, she used to be one of my regulars, but it's been a while—I barely recognized her. She'd been coming in since before I started. Pretty quiet usually, but get her on the right topic and she could gab all day. She liked knitting, and piano, and—if I remember right—bird watching. Yes, she was always with an older fellow. The man had a collection of Super Bowl sweatshirts he used to tell me all about. Fascinating, the things people collect. I've got a soft spot for those little puffballs with sticky feet myself. So cute.

But, this lady—I guess it's partly my fault. I read her all wrong. She wasn't at all like I remembered. When she set her basket of Lunchables on the belt, I figured she had kids. So I asked, but—but she said she didn't, and well, she looked pretty sad. It's never happened before—she didn't even seem interested in gabbing about the tabloids. What could I do? Whatever was making her blue, I thought I'd have a go at cheering her up.

So I said, "Glad to be done with work, I'll bet. Only

four days till T.G.I.F.!" But she only nodded and said she was retired.

I think she's lonely. The thing about this job is you learn so much about people. But it's not always sunshine, lollipops and rainbows. I kept at her, and she told me her whole life's story, practically. She's just retired, right after the passing of her father—rough thing, I ought to know—and she was gonna visit her sister in Florida, stay with her for a month. You gotta be with family in times like that. But, dear me, her sister died suddenly just as she was set to leave. Now what's she to do? I wish I had the answer. No family, no job, nothing to get her through the day. You know what she told me? She says to me, "What's the point of anything?" Me, I was ready to run over to the Kleenex aisle. Doesn't that just about kill you? Doesn't it just stab you in the heart and twist around in your chest? She goes to her doctor and all he does is give her pills without telling her what they are. She told me that.

Do you think she was crying out for help? I just feel I didn't do enough for her. Who am I, little old me behind this cash register, to pry. I guess she must be in a pretty bad way to have to tell all that to me. Probably she sensed my understanding personality. Happens a lot.

Before she left, the bearded gentleman behind her, the one who comes in every other day for cigarettes and liquor—and who, sorry, I don't much approve of—handed her a bottle of scotch. "You need this more than me," he said.

If there's one thing I can't stand it's eavesdroppers. And booze is certainly not the way we deal with personal issues. I hope you're not one of those girls who "hangs out" at those high school keg parties. Let me tell you, dear. If there's one thing boys look for in a girl, it's dignity, and you'll lose it if you partake of the "sauce." If you don't believe me, go have a chat with that homeless gentleman outside—he'll tell you all the wonders alcohol has done for him, I'm sure.

But anyway, you haven't complimented me on my new sweatshirt. "Love me, love my cat," it says, ha ha ha. Isn't that a hoot? The gals down at the senior center gave it to me, the sweet things. And boy, I don't know if there's a truer garment in my wardrobe. Tell me, do you have any pets?

That's all right, 'cause I got enough for both of us. Eight darlings—Rocko, Frisky Whiskers, Dumbo, Princess, Candy Cane, Monkey Feet, Talulah and Max. Not only a mouthful, but a handful and more, that's for sure! They're also a handful of love, and that's why I love 'em. My kids, I call 'em. Nope, never have been married. Maybe someday I'll meet that special someone—knock on wood—and who knows, he might be coming down this lane any minute. Yes sir, I'm getting up there in the years, but like I say: I've always considered myself an old soul—my body's just now getting caught up, ha ha! But seriously, when that mystery man asks me to take his hand there's just one thing I'm gonna say. Love me, love my cats!

Hmm. I wonder if a new kitten wouldn't do a world of good for that poor woman. My babies have gotten me through some rocky times—them and the Good Lord Himself, of course. I just can't help thinking I ought to do right for her. Maybe it's not my place. But if not me, who else? Oh, I just don't know. Why does there have to be so much sadness in the world?

All we can do is count on the nice little things to add up and make a difference. It's like my Uncle Maury, born without arms and legs, bless him. But just the nicest man regardless. Put up with a lot of strife since he was a boy, never let any of that turn him cold. When I was a little girl, he would take me all kinds of places—the circus, the ice rink, candy store, everywhere a little girl would dream of. Well, I guess you could say I was the one who took him. Course, people always stared. How they stared. Can't blame the little ones, 'cause they haven't learned better, but even some of the grownups—it rankles my hide to think of it. Like my mother used to say, just because he's got no arms to feel with doesn't mean he's got no feelings.

One day Maury took me over to the ice cream parlor. Nothing better when you're a kid than ice cream, right? John, the boy that worked there, well—gee, forty odd years on I'm still giggling about it. This boy John, I guess you could say I had a little crush on. And I'm ashamed of it now, but I was embarrassed for him to see me with Maury No-Arms—not my name, mind you, just what some of the bullies around town took to calling him. But John, bless his heart, treated Maury like a human being. Which is rarer than you'd want to think, back then. Gave us ice cream on the house, extra fudge. John even spoon-fed ol' Maury. Shoved the spoon in too hard and chipped a tooth, but oh well.

Just thinking of that random act of kindness, I figure it made me who I am today.

Not that I'm so special. People say I'm a people person. I say, everyone's a person, aren't they, so we should all be people persons—or people people, I guess I should say. No, that doesn't sound right.

Anyway, I think I will get in touch with the lady, if I can. Anything to help, and what a difference a smile makes. I just hope I'll be here the next time she shops. Those Lunchables can't last her that long. I don't know what it is. I've just got a feeling about this—

Hey, isn't it a little early to be going on your break?

WEDNESDAY

Dear, do you remember the code for Macintosh Apples? Oh, this would be much easier if only we had those—what are they called? Like rolodexes, you know? Anyway, I've been telling Big Al for months that we need some of those rolodex thingies with the PLU numbers in them to keep by the registers. But does he ever listen?

Not that I'm a gossip, but Suzanne—you know, the, how should I say, *snugly dressed* girl over in lane ten—she said some not so nice things to a customer the other day after a disagreement over the price of red grapes. Completely unprofessional. But did Big Al give her any grief about it? Course not. She just waved her you-know-whats around and Al was hypnotized. Disrespectful. A shame on the whole female gender, don't you think? I knew that Suzanne was trouble since—

By the way, you'll never guess who came back yesterday

afternoon. No, not Mr. Defranco. Are you even paying attention? That lady. Remember? The blue one, remember, I told you about her. "What's the point?" Her. For the second day in a row. Sometimes when you're lonely, it can be a comfort just to be in a public place, to be around people in any capacity.

Well, when I saw her coming down the aisle, I almost jumped over the register, let me tell you. But, nuts, the line here was six people deep, and I stood by as she went down to Suzanne's lane. Which, I guess I could admit, may be the reason why I'm so upset with her today. Color me the green-eyed monster.

But only because I want to help. Do you think the sad lady can count on Miss Priss to cheer her? Does Suzanne care one whit about the lasting effect she has on the lives of her customers—er, people? What difference does it make to Suzanne when she's given the opportunity to brighten that poor thing's day? I tell you, I get steamed when I think of the blah-blah way she greeted the lady, didn't even ask her how she was, didn't even care enough to ask if she preferred paper or plastic. Just assumed plastic.

Bet you didn't think I had this temper.

I can't help it. I just feel it's my calling. If I could I'd be a missionary or social worker—but maybe I'm needed here, in the everyday, where unfortunate people slip through the cracks. And believe me, it does happen. Why, I had a close girlfriend, Lorraine. I never felt I was there for her enough after her husband passed. In the end, she took to drinking. It got worse from there.

Sometimes I feel so helpless, so helpless that I—that I

just don't know what.

Yesterday I took my chance. I marched right up to that woman on her way out. Left my lane hanging, sure, but this was important. Did she remember me? Of course! Who could forget this bright red hair, ha! And it's no dye job, either, I swear on a Bible.

But this is serious. It's the little things. The little things you can do that make the difference. I believe that. "Dear," I said, "let me get your bags." And I took them right out of her hands. One thing you should know about people is that everyone needs to be touched now and then—not in a lewd way. I patted her on the shoulder and walked with her to her car. She didn't say much, mind you, but she was appreciative. I could tell.

Now I'm no Naïve Nancy. I've known pain. There are parts of life that just aren't easy for anyone. This woman, bundled in her coat like a lonely Eskimo, she was something else. You know what she said? She closes her door and says to me, "Thank you."

But it was the way she said it.

Every day you and me both walk by people, and maybe we don't give 'em a second thought. But what if we did? I've got a feeling about you, hon. You're kinda quiet. You stand there and bag and when you smile, it's like someone's got a gun to your head. I'm on to you. Seeing me the past few days, that's gotta make you think. I'm no Mother Theresa, but what did I say? Little things.

Oh, go ahead and roll your eyes at me. Because I know I'm loved. And I'm not afraid to love. And that lady, she just needs a little love. I can give that to her.

Don't go telling Big Al this, but I've got her address. Took it off the check she wrote. I think all she needs to know is that someone cares. I care. You must have had times when you felt like there was no one.

Now why would you call me a thing like that? I'm no stranger. This lady—and if you must know, her name is Claudine—she really opened up to me the other night. If we're not friends now, we will be. I was even thinking about rubbing Big Al's soft spot—not in a lewd way—get him to give her a job here in the lanes. Give her something to do, people to see. People who care.

You'll understand when you're older. What loneliness is. And it's not prying if it's sincere. I've taken heaps of adult ed. classes down at the center, even audited an intermediate psychology course or two. So believe me, I know what a cry for help sounds like.

That lady—Claudine—all she bought yesterday was soap and washing things. She must be a cleaner. I'm a baker-worrier myself. We've all got ways of dealing with stress. What I like to do—not to be morbid, but what I like to do is read the obituaries. Reminds me that everyone's life is significant. That's me, I look for the good in everyone. Claudine says she's no point in her life, well, then I'll find her one. Anybody deserves that. I don't care what you say.

THURSDAY

Anyone come in today to turn in a job form? 'Cause someone should be coming. That's right, I'm sure she'll be turning up any time now.

Oh, so now you want to know. Miss Cynical yesterday wants to know did I visit Claudine. I'll tell you, I did. Marched right over there after my shift.

Well, what do you want me to say? She lives alone. No pets—I told her she ought to get a couple of cats, but she's allergic. That's just too bad, I said to her. She shrugged. Shrugged a lot. Didn't feel much like talking, I guess. Sometimes it's enough just to have someone around. Sometimes you don't need to talk.

I forgot to say, before that—before she invited me in, it took some knocking. I knew she was home, could hear the TV. She must've fallen asleep on the couch. It took five minutes or more before she answered. But I'm persistent. Or maybe—I hate to say this, but—maybe she was ignoring me. Some people resist the things they know they need the most, just shut themselves up in their own little worlds.

When she answered the door I couldn't help but notice she was wearing the same clothes as last time. Come to think of it, she'd been wearing the same Super Bowl XX sweatshirt since Monday at least. It's normal for grooming habits to fall by the wayside during times of depression. My dear friend Lorraine wore the same sundress for three months after her husband passed. Poor thing, wasn't long before she—they buried her in that dress, alongside him.

"Sports fan?" I asked her. Claudine said no, not really. The sweatshirt had belonged to her dad. You see what I mean, then, about the grieving process?

So I looked Claudine in the eye. I said, "Hon, maybe

you don't know me so well." I said, "Maybe I don't know you so well. But gee, I think you need a friend as much as I'd like to be one."

You have to be bold, dear, to make a difference in our poor world.

So Claudine let me in. As soon as she opened that screen door more than a crack, I charged right inside. You've got to be a little forceful sometimes. The important thing is she opened the door.

Boy, if that house was any indication of what she feels like on the inside, then I couldn't have gotten there soon enough. The living room was—pardon me for saying it but it has to be said—a mess: dirty laundry piled on the furniture, a knocked-over houseplant and soil spilled all over the carpet, open pizza boxes on the floor, the pizza barely touched and at least two days old, Lunchables boxes.

But I won't go into details.

Claudine sat down on the couch. I sat down next to her, not forcing anything, just being there for her. We watched television together, one of those vulgar cops and murder programs. It was a little dark, so I turned on a lamp. But Claudine, she turned it right back off. It's natural for us to feed our dark moods with a dark atmosphere. Natural, but not right.

"What do you say we switch to a program a bit more cheery?" I said.

She shook her head.

"Have you eaten today?"

"Shh." She shushed me like that. "Shh," she said. "Haven't seen this one."

I can't say I wasn't disappointed. She was so talkative before, that first day at the checkout. But you gotta give people time to open up. It's a process. Friendships don't just happen.

When that horrid program was finally over, I leaned into poor Claudine and I'll tell you what I did. I took her hand, like this. I held it right there, like I had nothing else in the world to hold onto. And you know what happened? I felt it.

Dear, maybe you've never felt it before but I really hope one day you do. A feeling of charity, is the only way to describe it. It's heavenly. Like John, that day with Uncle Maury at the ice cream parlor.

"I've been thinking about what you said," I told her.

She turned off the sound on the television set, picked up a dirty sock that was stuck to the sofa's armrest and shrugged, and said yet again, "What's the point?"

And I hope never to hear that from you, dear. Those are the three worst words in the dictionary. What's the point? What *isn't* the point! I say. The fact that I'm here—that we're all here—that's the point.

Claudine kind of sneered at me—a sneer just like Suzanne's, come to think of it—and then she scratched herself in her—well, never mind that. It was then that I noticed the empty bottles stacked on the table.

So that's how it was. They don't call it the devil's apple juice for nothing.

Did I give up? No, I did not. It only showed me she needed me all the more. But you're going to say—I can tell by that kinda smug look in your eye (you think that'll attract a nice man, dear?)—that I stood there and lectured her like some grade school teacher. I bet that's what you think—

I'm sorry. I shouldn't talk to you like that. You're a great bagger and a nice, good girl, I'm sure. Not like Suzanne. I just get so worked up over this that my passion—no, my *com*passion—gets the better of me. So sorry. I was assuming, and you and I know it makes a donkey out of us both.

Anyway, where was I? Oh, yes. I'll tell you what I did—do I look a little tired today? Here's why. I cleaned Claudine's house. Yep, that's what I did. I cleaned, and I was up all night doing it. How many times have I said it? It's the little things. Those chores can overwhelm you, especially during hard times.

Now, we didn't talk much still. I asked her about her knitting and her bird watching, but all I got from her were shrugs and sighs. I vacuumed and scrubbed and dusted, and Claudine sat there on the couch with the television blaring. That didn't matter. I could tell by her eyes that she appreciated it. That she's gonna be all right from here on.

It's as simple as being a helping hand. And that's what I was—literally. Before I left, Claudine finally got up off the couch, and, well, I thought she was asking for a hug but she stepped past me and went into the bathroom. She came out with a pill bottle and—the meek little thing, her nerves are just shot to heck (pardon the French) from all the stress—her little fingers just couldn't untwist the cap. Darn things are pretty tricky, especially for old hands like mine, but by golly, I popped the thing open so that Claudine could take her medicine.

It was a sign, don't you see? She's ready to start the healing process. She *wants* to feel better. Gosh, I was so proud of Claudine that I held her tight in my big ol' arms and said, "Never forget, you sweet thing, that as long as you're on this Earth, people like me are gonna look out for you," and I told her to come by for groceries today and that I'd help her fill out an application. How do you like that?

In time she'll be ready to talk. I really do believe if everyone had a sit-down with someone like me, just a little chat about our feelings, then the world would be a pretty nice place. I'm no Miss Fix-It, tinkering with the lives of others. I'm more like a plumber, you know, unclogging the pipes. It's about expressing yourself, letting all of that beautiful, painful, ugly stuff out into the world. The Good Lord will hear you and take care of the rest. That I believe.

FRIDAY

I know, I know. I'm late. It's just that—I had a rough night. Look at these puffed-up eyes, dear. I'm not too much of a mess, am I? Normally I pride myself on my style, but today—today I'm just so sick and tired of—oh, I don't know.

So I guess you read the newspaper. How could someone do *that*? Such tragedy, and, oh, I had just gotten through to her. I don't believe it. Must have misread the label, or her doctor gave her the wrong pills. I just know in the heart of my heart of my heart that she didn't mean for it to happen.

Doctors these days, I don't know about them. They seem to be getting younger and younger. Why, I went in for a check-up the other day and that man couldn't have been a day older than seventeen. Who can you trust anymore? It rankles me to think that—

But I can't let myself get down this way. It's not what Lorraine would've wanted—it's not what Claudine would've wanted, either, bless her soul. If only she had reached out a little sooner. If only she'd given me a great big hug and asked me to stay the night with her, then maybe I could have prevented it. We've just gotta remind ourselves that it's times like these that make life life. What doesn't kill me makes me stronger—not physical strength, but the kind in your heart. We've got to continue loving, to bring happiness to everyone—even those, like that filthy man on the curb, who may not deserve it—because people like Claudine can't. I know she's up in Heaven laughing at what a fool she was. Because God forgives.

Why, I think I can hear her laugh in the chime of this cash register. Can't you, dear? It's a miracle. Praise God and all His—

Well hello there, Mr. Defranco. Paper or plastic?

And I Would've Gotten Away With It If It Wasn't For You Meddling Kids

In 1864 my Navajo ancestors were forcibly relocated from their homeland, *Dinétah*, and made to walk over three hundred miles to Bosque Redondo in the Pecos River Valley area of New Mexico, where they were held in a glorified internment camp and given access to scarcely enough food and supplies to survive. Four years later and after many hardships, the white man graciously declared the relocation a "failed experiment" and allowed my ancestors to return home, on foot.

Hundreds died on the way to Bosque Redondo and back, and now, here on the outskirts of Albuquerque—the rough halfway point of the Long Walk of the Navajo—I emerge from the secret cave entrance to the gold mine hidden behind this abandoned amusement park, wondering if it's my intuition or the spirits of my forebears that warns me of the garish van in the distance crawling along the gravelly road. Focusing my binoculars as the vehicle nears, I can just make out the words painted on its side: Mystery Machine.

I put on my mask, all bulging eyes, canine teeth and bloodstained fur, but then I change my mind, slip out of costume and back into coveralls. Better to not pull the spooks right off. Wouldn't want to pique their curiosity. I creep past the Barrel O'Fun Ferris Wheel and the other carnival rides, crawling on all fours to avoid being seen, past the Haunted Saloon and the Prairie Dog Concessions Stand and the ticket booth. When I reach the park gates they're already there, the Mystery Machine's headlights shining life into the burnt-out bulbs of the Cowboy Carousel. I crouch behind the marquee with the giant fluorescent letters that read Wild West World, and watch as the kids step out of the van, one by one.

There's three of them, a boy and two girls: a jock-looking type with yellow hair and a jaw line like JFK's; a curvy redhead in a purple dress; and a butch girl in a baggy orange sweater and thick, dark glasses. Maybe it *was* my ancestors warning me, but I don't believe in that bullshit, anyway. One look at my costume and these kids'll run like all the others, and I'll be left alone to finish my work.

The jock looks around, turns to the girls and says, "This must be the place, gang."

The redhead nods, candy-pink lips parted. "It sure is, Fred! And my Grandpa Willie was right. Things seem pretty mysterious around here."

Thumbs in the back pockets of his bellbottoms, the jock says, "Good thing Daphne's grandpa hired us to investigate the mystery of the abandoned amusement park, eh, Velma?"

"Yeah, Fred, sure." The butch one scowls and spits in the dirt. "I wonder how this one's gonna end up. Maybe exactly like all the others, you think?"

There's more of them. Someone's pounding on the van's back door. "Like, let us outta here, man. Door's stuck and we're starving!" The butch one unlocks the trunk and they practically fall out, a goateed burnout and his dog—

looks like a Great Dane, like Marmaduke from the Sunday Funnies. "Hey, man, like, this ain't like no diner."

The jock pats the burnout on his back. "There's no time for that, Shaggy. If there really is a ghost around here like Grandpa Willie says, then we've got to get to the bottom of it."

"All right, man, but tell that to Scooby." The burnout looks at the dog as if it were talking to him, but the dog only licks itself and sniffs the dirt. The burnout replies, "I know what you mean, Scoob." Butch rolls her eyes and slaps her forehead.

I spit on my hands and rub my face, and when I'm sure I've cleaned away any remaining rock dust, I stand up and approach the kids. "Howdy, folks," I say in my friendliest, for-the-tourists voice, the one that makes white people feel like I'm the Tonto to their Lone Rangers.

The burnout, who looks like he's suffering some kind of hallucination, leaps into the air and lands on his ass. "Cool down, Shaggy," the jock says. "It's only Old Man Nakai, the groundskeeper."

"But like, Fred, he don't look so old to me."

"It's only my Indian name, Kemo Sabe." I smile. "I can guess what brings you folks to these parts. I must warn you, I've seen the monster myself."

The burnout leans down and whispers in the dog's ear, "Like, did he just say m-m-m-m-m-m-monster?" He nods in agreement, but all the dog does is lick its asshole.

"*Yee naaldlooshii*," I say. "Navajo for 'With it, he goes on all fours.' Skinwalker. Werewolf." I shrug. "It's what happens when you build an amusement park over ancient

Indian burial grounds." The same lie I told Mr. Blake when I sold him the park.

The redhead rests her hand on her round hip and looks me over. "Funny, I thought Grandpa Willie said you didn't work for him anymore, ever since the monster scared away all the business and the park had to close."

"You're Mr. Blake's niece, then," I say. "You're mistaken." It's not until this moment that I realize I've still got my pickaxe in hand, that I'm pointing it at her throat. I lean it against the fence. "Just a prop," I explain. "Well, I've got work to do. Grounds don't keep themselves, you know. You kids feel free to look around. But don't say I didn't warn you."

I leave them, head slowly back into the park. I'll hide somewhere they can't see me and watch, ensure that they don't enter the caves and discover the secret gold mine, in which I pick out my fortune the old-fashioned way, nugget by nugget. TNT would attract too much attention.

Behind me I hear the jock: "Come on, gang. There's gotta be a clue around here somewhere. We'll crack this case in no time."

"Yes," says the butch one. "Oh, how I wonder who could be responsible for this."

Something tickles my neck, but there's nothing there. Maybe it's the vengeful spirits of my ancestors, or just the wind, but I have a feeling it's the hot, suspicious gaze of the butch girl, magnified by those Coke-bottle lenses.

※

It was to be called Navajo Nation, America's first Native American-themed amusement park. Even as I walk the grounds of the Wild West World it became, I imagine it as it should have been. Here, where the Haunted Saloon stands, was supposed to be the Navajo Achievement and Long Walk Memorial Museum, with full food court and gift shop. In place of the Big Rez Hide & Seek Playground, Mr. Blake installed the Wild West Shoot 'Em Up gallery, of which one of the objectives is to shoot the feathers off a cigar store Indian's head with a BB gun. The walls of the arena that should've hosted my traditional Navajo music and dance stage show are plastered now with posters and fliers advertising rodeos and square dances. Even the carousel was repurposed for the western theme: cowboy hats and six-shooters for each horse and, painted along the sides, a pictorial narrative of some brave cartoon cowboys chasing away a band of cowardly redskins.

I'd dreamt of it since I was a boy. I used to draw blueprints for rides and attractions in the margins of my school notebooks. I told anyone who asked that what I wanted to be when I grew up was an amusement park owner. Not just any amusement park, but Navajo Nation, a special, one-of-a-kind park whose centerpiece would be an authentic recreation of an ancient Navajo village, a park that would be more fun than Disneyland, a park that would bring pride to my people.

After all the trouble, after the false starts and the standstills, after the bankruptcy, after Charlie screwed me, when I'd finally given up on the park and sold the land to Mr. Blake, the first thing he did was commission a statue of Kit Carson to set by the water fountains. "No offense, son," he said, "but you've got to know your customers.

This Indian shit is depressing." Then he offered me the job as groundskeeper, said my face would "bring color to the atmosphere."

The kids have split up now. Atop the Ferris wheel, I watch through the pinhole eyes of my mask as the jock and the redhead begin to walk the perimeter of the performance arena while the burnout, the butch girl, and the dog enter through the swinging doors of the Haunted Saloon.

I have to admit part of me enjoys it, the thrill of the hunt, the tingle of anticipation. When I was a kid I used to sneak out at night and wander the Rez, looking in other people's houses. With the lights on, the glass of the windows glowed like television screens. I felt invited, invisible, like I could walk inside and do whatever I wanted and nobody could stop me. I felt outside of my body, like a spirit.

The jock and the redhead are so near that I think I can hear their breathing even from up here. The redhead looks over her shoulder. For a moment I fear she senses me, but then I realize she's only checking if the coast is clear. When she sees that she and the jock are alone she grabs his hips and pins him against a concessions stand. Giggling, she kisses him, sliding her tongue across his neck, creeping her fingers down his pants. "C'mon, Daphne," he sighs, lightly batting her hand. "Quit fooling around. We've got a mystery to solve."

"Can it, Fred. You know you want it." She lifts her skirt and unbuckles his belt.

"But think of the clues we could be finding. Say, are those footprints over there? We ought to—ummmph." She cups his mouth with one hand and, as he squirms, digs the other into his underwear.

They won't be any more vulnerable than they are now. I start my climb down, pausing for a moment by the seat I carved my initials into the day of Navajo Nation's official groundbreaking ceremony. I see the picture in my mind and can hardly recognize myself without my costume on.

But here I am, like a kid on Halloween, creeping up on a couple of horny teenagers too busy going at it to notice me. The redhead crouches before the jock, her head bouncing up and down like a galloping horse, while he blushes and mutters, "I'm just not in the mood right now, okay? Think of the mystery."

I flail my arms and try my best Bela Lugosi impression. "Leave this plaa-ace! Leave! You have disturbed the spirits and you must paa-aay!" I get on all fours and growl, slicing my claws through the air. Guess it's one thing Charlie and I now have in common; we're both good at playing villains.

"Yikes!" The jock takes one look at me, pushes the redhead into the dirt and bolts, tripping on his underwear as he goes. Sprinting, his pecker wagging before him, he calls back, "Run for your life, Daphne!" The redhead screams and skitters after so fast that it's like her legs are struggling to keep up with the rest of her. Her bra is left hanging on the stand's countertop like a flag of surrender.

Two down, three to go. I sneak back to the cave and crawl into the secret tunnel that runs under the Haunted Saloon.

🛸

The theme park was on my mind as I left home for college,

and it was what pushed me to graduate at the top of my class at BYU's Marriot School. After graduation, I returned home with only student debt and the idea I'd started with. Gone were the child's colorful, crayon-drawn blueprints, gone were the idle daydreams of my youth. I now had a sound business plan and real ambition, but that was it. All the promising contacts I'd made in business school were suddenly useless. The few potential investors who'd take my calls all stopped me at "Navajo theme park." It was too niche, they said, too risky. Couldn't I tweak it, make it more mainstream?

I didn't let that stop me. I sent letters, I telephoned, I shamelessly begged every friend and relative in my extended personal network who might have money. After months of dead ends, a friend of a friend of a college buddy who was working in Hollywood put me in touch with my estranged Great Uncle Charlie, who I'd heard about but had never met. Charlie had never married, had no kids, hadn't lived in the homeland since he was twelve years old. I think he liked to think of me as a kind of son. At least, that's what I convinced myself at the time.

Just weeks after our first phone call, Great Uncle Charlie arrived in his private jet at the Albuquerque airport. I was there to receive him at the gate when he promptly blindfolded me, sat me in the passenger seat of his rented car and drove me I-didn't-know-where. When finally he lifted the blindfold, I was here. Nothing but empty desert, but I knew before he said a word that it was *my* empty desert. "Well, what do you think?" he said. "Will it do?"

Charlie was an actor in the forties and fifties. Had

bit parts in over sixty movies, all westerns, and he never played a character who wasn't named "Indian," "Chief," or "Scout." In his mansion there hangs a photograph on the living room wall of him shaking hands with John Wayne. Charlie didn't make much money as an actor, but he invested it well, started his own production company and became a multimillionaire before he turned thirty. Now he was investing in me, gifting me the land on which I'd build my park and, as Navajo Nation's newly appointed Chief Financial Officer, using his connections to accrue the necessary funds to get the park up and running.

"Uncle Charlie," I said, "we're blazing trails here. This park is a monument to our nation."

"Well, there's that," Charlie said. "But more important, we're gonna make a hell of a lot of money."

🛸

Eyes in perfect alignment with the holes I've carved out of the portrait of Billy the Kid, my pupils follow the burnout as he passes by the bar in the Haunted Saloon. "Like, even cowboys gotta eat, right, man? Must be some grub around here somewhere." He looks above the bar but only finds empty prop bottles. Meanwhile, the dog mounts a wax statue of a gunfighter, his paw slipping onto the button that triggers the animatronics show. The curtains part on the saloon stage and the dancing girls hum to life, kicking their steel legs in unison as the player piano begins its tune. "Zoinks!" Startled, the burnout leaps behind the bar and cowers.

When the song ends and the curtains close, he looks over the edge. He sighs and wipes his head. "Like, would you look at that? I thought I was freaking out, but it's just part of the show, eh, Scoob? Scoob?" Finished with the statue, the dog goes to his master and sniffs around. I take the opportunity to sound some spooky oooohs and aaaahs through the saloon's PA, cranking the reverb up to the max. "Like, where did that come from?"

Back behind the painting I roll my eyes as the burnout scans the shelves on the walls. He freezes, looks at the painting, looks at the dog, looks back at the painting. I blink. He tugs on the dog's collar. "Zoinks! Like, did you just see what I saw?"

The dog growls, nips his fingers. I push the painting out from the wall and reveal myself. I dive through the opening and scratch at them with my rubber claws. "Leave this place!" I moan. "Lea-aa-ve at once!"

"Like, this ain't no cow*boy*, Scoob, it's a man—a *wolf*man!" He runs in place, practically levitating in the air, his feet pattering like bongo drums, then zips over the card tables and through the swinging doors, leaving a cloud of dust in his wake.

The dog howls fiercely and jumps me. I fall to the floor under its surprising weight. Its claws dig into my shoulders, tearing the fabric of my costume. I roll, throw the mutt off of me, slapping its eyes, but it bites my costume hand and won't let go. I kick with as much force as I can muster but its teeth remain clenched. Finally, the dog tears the claw from my bare hand and trots away satisfied.

"Shaggy? Scooby? Where are you?" A voice from outside—the butch girl, the smartest of the bunch. I pull the lever under the bar that opens the secret door in the wall, put the painting back in place, and wait.

⚊

It didn't take long for my Great Uncle Charlie to round up investors for my park. Working in an office Charlie rented in Albuquerque, I'd meanwhile applied for the necessary permits, completed the paperwork and begun hiring crews for construction. Tedious, brainless work—founding Navajo Nation wasn't the way I'd dreamed it as a boy. I worked for months in that cramped office without air conditioning, arriving every morning at seven and working late into the night. I didn't even have time to visit the land on which my dreams would soon be realized, though sometimes late at night, when I was half-asleep at my desk, I thought I could hear the bones of my ancestors calling to me from miles away.

On groundbreaking day I arrived at the future site of Navajo Nation to find Charlie waiting for me, a carousel and a towering Ferris wheel where the park plans stipulated the welcome center should be. "What do you think, boy? Isn't it something already?"

"I don't understand," I said. I removed the plans I carried with me in a canister and laid them flat on the desert ground, pointing to the area clearly labeled Welcome Center.

Charlie grinned. "That's only a draft, my boy. This is called development. You wanna attract customers, you gotta have spectacle, rides, theatrics. Wait'll you see it after we put in the roller coaster."

I couldn't argue with him. After all, he was the real businessman and it was his money. Let people come for facile carnival rides, I thought as I dug my shovel ceremoniously into the dirt, the photographers snapping my picture. They'll stay for the deeper thrill of Little *Dinétah*, my reverent simulation of a pre-Columbian Navajo village.

Construction continued. Anticipation grew. The photos of the groundbreaking ceremony made the front page of the business section that week. A towering billboard was constructed. Welcome to the future site of Navajo Nation, it declared in letters arranged out of cartoon tomahawks.

Months later Navajo Nation was in the news again, this time on the front page. The roller coaster Charlie had talked me into building had collapsed during its first test run, killing a couple of construction workers who'd agreed to serve as crash dummies for a few extra bucks in their paycheck. Charlie, acting as de facto publicist, called it an "act of God" but it was no doubt the faulty bearings he'd bought on discount from a less than reputable wholesaler from Mexico. He'd been cutting costs from the beginning, fudging the books and pocketing the money saved. Fearing the inevitable public scandal and lawsuits, the investors pulled out immediately.

That was it. I put everything I had into Navajo Nation and lost it all instantly. I had no choice but to sell the land to Mr. Blake at a fraction of its worth. As I signed the deed over, I told him some bullshit story about the park being built on consecrated ground, about cursed land and the spirits of vengeful Navajo witches. He smirked and said, "I'll take my chances."

Soon after, I learned that Charlie was Wild West

World's biggest investor. "Sorry," he told me, "but business is business."

The butch girl enters the saloon. Her flashlight beam a blazing beacon in the darkness, it takes my eyes a moment to adjust before I can watch, safe behind this painting, as she stumbles around the cobwebbed card tables and cowboy dummies. "Scooby!" she calls. "Shagg—aw, screw it." She reaches into her pocket and pulls out a packet of nicotine gum. There's only one piece left. "Jinkies," she huffs. Stomping her feet, she trips the button and starts the animatronics show again. "Goddamn jinkies. This is just what I need." She sits cross-legged on the floor and gazes up at the mechanical dancing ladies on stage. "'Velma,' they said, 'why would you want to drive around the country solving mysteries with three hippies and a flea-ridden mutt?' Christ, what I must have been thinking. I dropped out of Cornell for *this*?" She sticks the gum under the table, reaches into her pocket and pulls out a pack of cigarettes.

I punch the painting off the wall, lean out and growl, "Curse you! Curse you, and leave this place now!" She stands but doesn't run, so I climb through the wall and corner her, hiding my exposed hand behind my back.

She sighs, clenches her teeth, then lunges at my neck, throttling me with surprisingly brawny hands. I try to squirm out of her grasp but my mask, caught between her fingers, begins to peel away. "Come on," she says, "get this thing off so I can go home and, ugh," I grab her wrist and squeeze, "take a bath." She kicks now, throws her fist haphazardly, her face flushing red. "I know it's you," she says. "Obvious. Old Man Nakai."

How could she have seen through my clever ruse?

Roaring, I slam the girl against the wall. Her arms fold in on her chest, and she opens her mouth to speak, to scream. I twist her sweater around my bare hand, reach back with my rubber claw and pound her head against a jagged nail in the wall. The blood, her broken glasses, her whimpering, it only makes me want to hurt her more. I push her down, watch her body crumple as I reach under the bar for a heavy glass jug. I imagine a shattering sound as the jug cracks her skull, but it's merely a dull thud, and when I'm finished the jug isn't even chipped. The girl lies motionless, her glasses splintered, her Beatles hair caked with blood.

Oh god, not again! What have I done!

⏢

If I couldn't have Navajo Nation, I was going to make damn sure that "Grandpa" Willie Blake's Wild West World wouldn't succeed in its place. Although its grand opening drew record crowds, things quickly went south. Rides frequently malfunctioned and broke down, even after they'd been service-tested and safety-checked by numerous technicians. Customers complained of whiplash and broken bones. The shattered lights of the performance arena were attributed to vandals, as was the damaged air-conditioning system. Attendance levels sunk drastically as the summer wore on, bolstered by strange rumors of haunted rides and buildings, of evil presences, of children gone mysteriously missing.

It was me, of course. I'd taken the job of groundskeeper

in order to sabotage the park from the inside. You'd have thought that Mr. Blake would've suspected me, but for that he would've had to see me as a person more than Tonto, his docile Indian servant. He actually called me that. Tonto do this, Tonto do that. "Tonto, go spread some sawdust on cart 3 in Bumper Wagons. Well come on, get going. Hi-yo, away!" He never even knew my real name.

The customers were worse. I was another mascot to them, like the guys who walked around in felt costumes dressed as Twinkie the Kid and Sheriff Hot Dog. Families crowded me as I walked my rounds. They stood their kids next to me and snapped photos of a real live Indian. They lined up as they would before a mall Santa Claus, demanding to hear some sage Indian wisdom, some funny Indian legends.

So I told them. I told them about the ancient Indian burial ground the park was built on, about the angry spirits that haunted the land. The customers would laugh and pat my back like it was all part of the show, but I'd look them in the eye and pound my fist into my palm so they'd know I was serious.

It was just reheated Navajo folklore, stories you'd hear from a shrewd salesman at any chintzy Indian crafts fair, where the yuppie customers nod and look interested, so proud of themselves for appreciating such weird, savage culture that they purchase jewelry at ten times the retail price. Digging through the recesses of my mind, thinking back to picture books I'd read as a boy, the tall tales and ghost stories passed from one neighborhood kid to another, I spoke, surely getting the details mixed up—not that it mattered—of the Witchery Way, of evil Navajo witches whose dark powers are ignited by the murder of a close relative, of shapeshifting skinwalkers who assume the likenesses of animals. The funny thing is, after a while, they believed me.

Well, I suppose it helped that I'd taken to stalking the park at night dressed as a ferocious werewolf, chasing away customers and stoking the coals of superstition. Wild West World had been built with the skeleton of my plans for Navajo Nation and without much of Mr. Blake's direct supervision, so only I knew of the vast system of secret tunnels that run under the park and connect each building. As I crept along the grounds and through the tunnels at night, I could almost hear my ancestors cackling in the wind, imitating the cartoon spooks people saw in them. Not that I believed any of that crap. Still, my land had been taken from me, and so I waged a war, a war not unlike the one that failed my ancestors many years ago and sent them on the walk to Bosque Redondo.

It was on one of my night stalks that I discovered the secret gold mine in a cave on the periphery of the park grounds. From the beginning I'd used the cave to change unnoticed into costume, but it wasn't until I dropped my flashlight one night while slipping on my wolf claw that I knew of the fortune in my grasp; the flashlight rolled, hit a rock, sending the beam into a patch of shimmering specks in the cave wall.

Now I had a reason other than petty revenge for driving the people away. I could harvest the gold and use the money I'd make to independently fund my Navajo Nation.

I'd have complete control over the park, and if I accrued enough gold, I'd have enough money that I wouldn't have to worry about compromising my dream for the sake of profit. My Navajo Nation would have no kitschy rides, no grubby hot dog stands, no guys in ugly felt costumes, only an authentic recreation of a pre-Columbian Navajo village and a tasteful playground for the kids.

Although Mr. Blake beefed up security, the guards ran faster than anyone. Once again, the investors pulled out, one by one this time, until only Charlie was left. The park was shut down—Mr. Blake insisted it was only for scheduled maintenance—and with the grounds all but abandoned, I could mine the gold without disturbance.

⊶⊷

I swore it would never happen again, that it was all only pretend, but just now, as I killed the girl, I felt something in me transform, as if the blood in my veins reversed its flow. I was hardly conscious of my movements until it was too late.

I open my eyes and the girl is already dead. I drag her body into the Haunted Saloon's maintenance closet. Behind the bags of sawdust there's a hidden lever that reveals the trapdoor to the tunnels. I open it and drop the body, listen as it lifelessly slaps the tunnel's cement floor. "She fell." I don't know why I say it aloud. "She fell, and her head hit a rock."

I must reach the caves before they get me. I haven't harvested as much gold as I'd intended, but what I've stored there will do. Enough to buy a plot of land, at least, and construct the basic village. What transpired is regrettable, but it'd only be unfair to Navajo Nation, to my ancestors, if I were locked away.

Can't take the tunnel and risk implicating myself in the girl's death. It's Mr. Blake's property, ergo his tunnels. I'm just the harmless Indian maintenance guy. I know nothing of any tunnels. What secret tunnels? Looks to me like the girl fell.

I creep outside, the kids' voices distant, muffled, carried by the wind. I turn at the Ferris wheel, careful to remain under shadow, and then follow the perimeter of the performance arena. The cave is far but in my line of sight when three flashlight beams spotlight me.

I mean to moan "Leave this place" again but what comes out is a bestial, guttural growl. I can't see them—damn the pinhole eyes of this mask—but they're close, so close I can almost feel the dog's moist breath on my ankles. There's no other way, I rush through the entrance of the performance arena and down the vast corridors, feet and light beams trailing behind me. If I can reach the fire exit, the cave isn't far. Attempting to lose the kids, I run in one door and out the other, in one and out the other, like an old Marx brothers gag, and the kids follow. They split up, each to a different door, and wind up colliding back in the hall.

The night cloaks me and the fire alarms howl as I push through the exit. My senses heightened, I rush to the golden glow that awaits me in the cave. I'm a monster, I remind myself, and growl some more.

From behind: "C'mon, gang! Let's get him!"

Branches whip me as I run, sharp stones poke my feet,

but I feel nothing. I gallop on all fours, feel more powerful than ever, more animal than man. Yes, I'll do what needs to be done. I'll get my gold and found my park, but more importantly, I'll have my revenge. These kids, walking all over my land like they're entitled to it, I'll show them what I'm capable of.

I howl once more. I am wolf-spirit made corporeal: limbering, my sinews tense, the sweet, metallic scent of blood filling my nostrils.

"There he goes, Fred! Don't lose him."

"Like, we'll wait here, man."

Woof! Woof!

Their voices are closer now. No matter, I reach the black maw of the cave, head straight for the crates where I've stored what's rightfully mine. I step forward, something clenches my ankle and suddenly I am looking up at the ground, blood sinking from my toes into my head. My body, it's only an impotent man's. My skin, my fur, my teeth—it's just a costume. I don't know how much time passes before their lights shine on me. One of them—I'm too tired to even look—says, "Now let's see who you *really* are." Blackness.

The first time it happened, I told myself it was an accident. I was in the cave, pickaxe in hand, costume on except for the mask. A particularly large chunk of gold hung loose in the cave wall like a baby tooth, and I was just about to extract it when a voice crept in from behind. "Boy, what the hell do you think you're doing?"

I turned. "Uncle, what are you doing here?"

Charlie frowned, but it wasn't a real frown—exaggerated, cartoonish, an actor's expression. I remembered it from the anti-littering public service announcement. All he was missing was a glycerin tear. "I own half this land and you're asking *me*?" His speech was automatic. He wasn't looking at me. His eyes were on my costume. "So you're the one. Running around like a goddamn kid and spooking folks out of my business."

I lifted the pickaxe, dug it into the wall. The gold nugget dropped onto the cave floor. I picked it up and held it in my palm. "Don't you see? It goes deep, I think, back layers and layers. We can use it, Uncle. We don't need investors. We won't even have to worry about making a profit. Buy the rest of the land back and Navajo Nation can be self-sustaining."

The gold speckled in the surfaces of his eyes. "Oh." Hypnotized by it, he shook his head and scoffed, pinching the fur of my costume with his two fingers. "A nonprofit amusement park? You damn fool. When Blake hears about this—"

That was the first time. My body left me for a moment and this rubber suit was my real skin. I was the monster. My thoughts, my fears, my regrets were swallowed into its soulless heart. When my body returned to me, Charlie was scrunched in the dirt, the gold casting a yellow glow in his eyes, the pickaxe sticking out of his skull like a flagpole.

When I awake I'm shackled in handcuffs outside the park entrance. The red and blue lights of the squad car flash carnival colors over the attractions. Looking at it reminds me of a time when people flocked here, when I'd stroll the premises of Navajo Nation and greet every boy and girl with a smile and a wink. That never really happened, but it's how I pictured it.

The kids—the jock, the redhead, the burnout—stand with their dog, talking to two police officers. "...and when we found this pickaxe Old Man Nakai left out, Daphne couldn't help but notice the flecks of gold on it..."

"So it was only a matter of time before we stumbled into the cave and found the decomposing corpse of Uncle Charlie and the trail of footprints that led right to the mines."

"Like, it was me and Scooby who stumbled into it. We thought we smelled chicken nuggets, man, but they were just *gold* nuggets." He hands the nugget to one of the officers, who seals it in plastic bag marked Evidence.

The redhead puts her arm around the jock's waist. "Now my Grandpa Willie will have enough money to keep the park open forever!"

"We caught him just in time, too. Old Man Nakai was about to make off with the loot."

And why shouldn't I say it? I was a good man once, circumstances changed me. This group of kids and their dog took from me my humanity. I no longer have my mask, but still, I'll be the monster they expect me to be. I stomp my feet in the dirt, letting the words flow through me, words perhaps not unlike those spoken by the United States government to Chief Barboncito the day they conceded and issued the Navajo Treaty of 1868:

"And I would've gotten away with it if it wasn't for you

meddling kids!"

The cops shove me into the back of their squad car. I put my face against the window and sneer.

"Like, I guess this werewolf was nothing more than a were-wannabe, eh, Scooby?"

The dog rolls onto his back and guffaws, "Ruff! Ahehehehe!" They're all laughing, loud and long, in an almost impatient way, as if they're waiting for the closing credits to roll. They laugh, even as behind them two more police officers roll the body bag out of the Haunted Saloon on a stretcher.

And what becomes of the Mystery Machine gang now, this callous tribe that can stand around and crack jokes even after the loss of one of their own? They'll replace her, with a scrappy young sidekick pup, possibly, or the burnout's long lost, southern-accented cousin. It's no matter to them. They will go on as always, solve mystery after mystery, the pursuit never ending, every case a restart, a new beginning. A syndicated life, no conflict ever truly resolved. And what of me, the dastardly villain Old Man Nakai? My story is only history. My story is over.

Acknowledgements

Some of these stories have appeared, in slightly different form, in the following publications: "Surfer Girl," *Hayden's Ferry Review*; "He's a Rebel," *Mid American Review*; "Mom's Team v. Dad's Team," *Versal*; "Betty and Veronica," *Gargoyle*; "The Party Don't Stop," *Washington Square Review*; "Invasion" and "Bongo the Space Ape," *Pank*; "Another Girl, Another Planet," *Conjunctions*; "The Enormous Television Set," *roger: an art and literary magazine*; "Defunct Girl Gangs of North American Drive-Ins," *The Collagist*; and "And I Would've Gotten Away With It If It Wasn't For You Meddling Kids," *Jabberwock Review*. Sincerest thanks to the editors of these journals, especially Beth Staples and Richard Peabody, of *Hayden's Ferry Review* and *Gargoyle* respectively, who have been particularly supportive of my work and particularly kind to me personally, and whose acceptances marked drastic turning points in my writing career.

Thank you to Woody Skinner, Ian Golding, Richard Klein, and my best friend, Daisy Carlsen. I am not someone who is easy to get to know, and this book would probably not exist—and I would not exist—if you hadn't forced me to get to know you.

Thank you to my teachers and friends at the University of Wisconsin, Oshkosh, and the University of Cincinnati.

Thank you to Quentin S. Crisp for opening up space in which this weird book can exist and for shepherding it to publication with wisdom and care. I wish you endless dreams of Annette Funicello.

And finally, deepest gratitude is owed to Steph Barnard, who keeps me from being eaten alive by my own neuroses, and who loves me—for some reason—unconditionally.

About the Author

Luke Geddes was born and grew up in Appleton, Wisconsin. His stories have appeared in *Hayden's Ferry Review*, *Conjunctions*, *Mid American Review*, and other journals. He currently lives in Cincinnati, Ohio, with his girlfriend, Steph, and their cat, Talulah Gosh. This is his first book.

Also from Chômu Press:

Looking for something else to read? Want a book that will wake you up, not put you to sleep?

The Secret Life of the Panda
By Nick Jackson

I Wonder What Human Flesh Tastes Like
By Justin Isis

Jeanette
By Joe Simpson Walker

The Life of Polycrates and Other Stories for Antiquated Children
By Brendan Connell

Nemonymous Night
By D.F. Lewis

"Remember You're a One-Ball!"
By Quentin S. Crisp

Here Comes the Nice
By Jeremy Reed

For more information about these books and others, please visit: http://chomupress.com/

Subscribe to our mailing list for updates and exclusive rarities.

CPSIA information can be obtained at www.ICGtesting.com
Printed in the USA
LVOW082024120213

319791LV00001B/19/P